THE FIRST CHILL OF AUTUMN

SHARDS OF A BROKEN SWORD, BOOK THREE

W.R. GINGELL

*For my mother. She loves **Playing Hearts** best of all but the dedication for that one was already taken so she has to put up with this one instead.*

Sorry, Ma.

THE SUMMER OF YOUTH

*U*ntil she reached the age of seventeen there were four certainties in the life of Dion ferch Alawn.

The first was that her parents were always wise, always right.

The second was that her life would always fall into the same orderly rhythms as it had thus far.

Thirdly, she had no doubt that she would one day be queen.

The fourth thing of which Dion ferch Alawn was absolutely certain was that the tall, ebony-skinned man she saw in her bedroom mirror meant her no harm.

As it turned out, this was the only thing in which she was entirely correct.

DION WAS three when the Fae arrived. She watched the first stately audience from the Upper Gallery as the Fae swept gracefully through the Audience Hall below, tall, graceful people with beautifully tragic faces. She felt her nurse's fingers pinching at her shoulder and knew she was being reminded not to gape and point. Dion knew dimly that it was a Very Bad Thing for the Princess Heir to gape and point. She wished she could be as free as her twin sister Aerwn, who didn't care about the nurse's pinching fingers, and gaped and gasped and bounced to her heart's content.

The Fae came in small numbers at first, fleeing from a peril in Faery that was talked about in hushed tones. *The Guardians* were said to be Fae of the worst kind; beast-like warmongers who had already taken over much of Faery. Dion heard the whispers, but never much more than whispers, despite her awe-struck observation of the Fae who arrived from week to week. The homeless Fae each asked for and were granted an audience with the King and Queen, and most were settled in Harlech. Dion also heard the mutters around the castle when it became known that the Crown—and by proxy the people—were paying for their resettlement and daily food.

Before long there was a steady stream of Fae arriving every day. Some of them settled in Harlech, some in other Llassarian cities, and still more of them moved right in the castle itself. Soon the maids were all Fae, swiftly and gracefully performing their duties. The footmen morphed from a group of well-trained and orderly men into a regiment of perfectly starched, perfectly beautiful Fae.

By the time Dion and Aerwn were five, their tutors were all Fae. Aerwn, naturally graceful and quick to learn, blossomed beautifully under their tutelage. Dion, who always felt clumsy and awkward around the Fae, felt herself becoming even more stiff, careful, and silent. Despite that, she discovered that the Fae had a great deal to teach even her. She didn't find that she grew more graceful or more silver-tongued, like Aerwn, but she did begin to learn that there were other things in which she could excel. The Fae, upon learning that Dion had a decided talent for magic, patted her on the head and gave her spells to learn. She applied herself assiduously, and had the pleasure of feeling that she had surprised her tutors when she effortlessly performed the spells for them. Dion thought that they were a little more careful with the spells they gave her to learn after that, but they didn't stop giving her spells, and before long she had her own Instructor of Magic.

DION HAD BECOME SO USED to the constant presence of the Fae in her life that when the tall, black Fae first appeared in her oval dressing mirror, she didn't think more of it than to feel in a vaguely embarrassed way that she was the one who was intruding. After all, Fae were free to come and go wherever they pleased, and Dion knew not to question or challenge the Fae rudely.

Fae thoughts are high and wise, she knew. *A Fae always has a reason for what the Fae does. It is not for mortals to question or upbraid.*

So Dion hurried past her mirror whenever she was in her suite, hastily averting her eyes whenever she saw that the tall Fae was back. She was so used to being observed and tested by then that being watched even in her suite didn't seem unusual. And the Fae, apart from the fact of his actual presence, wasn't intrusive. He didn't do much more than stand there, though sometimes he seemed to be talking. Since no sound came through the glass, Dion assumed that he was talking to other Fae on his side of the mirror, and still abashedly avoided it as much as she could.

A FEW MONTHS after her seventh birthday, Dion sprained her ankle. If she was really honest about it, thought Dion, as with most things in the twins' lives, it wasn't so much that she had sprained her ankle, but that Aerwn had sprained it for her. It was Aerwn who had bullied her into climbing into the saddle of their father's horse; Aerwn who confidently asserted that she could and would climb on *right after you, you scardy!*; Aerwn who had opened the stable door for them both; Aerwn who seized upon

Dion's foot when their father's horse charged grimly for freedom, dashing herself and her sister to the unforgiving paving-stones of the stable.

And of course it was Dion who finished the day in bed, her face whiter than usual and her sprained foot very carefully elevated. The Fae were too sensible to heal human injuries quickly without reason—Dion herself had been taught how dangerous it was for the human system to be brought to rely upon magic for its healing—and she had been put to bed for the afternoon with the promise that she would be better tomorrow.

It was only after the solicitous rush had dissipated and Dion's nurse had withdrawn to the next room that Dion saw her dressing mirror had been angled so as to give her a reflected view of the outside world. Or it would have done, if the tall man wasn't reflecting still more strongly from the glass. Someone must have done it in a spirit of kindness, but Dion wished they hadn't made the effort, because it meant an agony of embarrassment in her attempts not to look at it. First she gazed at the gauzy sweeps of her canopy, then toward the window; now at her bedposts and then at her toes. Looking at her toes had the unfortunate result of bringing her into direct eye contact with the man in the mirror, however, and Dion looked away awkwardly. At last she settled on pretending to read a book, her face carefully shielded from the mirror; and began to feel the stiffness in her cheeks relax a little. Dion liked reading, though if poetry were excluded, there weren't really many books to read for pleasure. Previously popular books, with their old prejudices and ancient enmity, were frowned upon by the king and queen. The castle had once had such books, Dion knew, but with the Fae had come the Cleansing: the washing away of all previous conflicts and anything that could be used to incite unrest. It was necessary. But Dion remembered some of the tales that had been read to her only a few years ago, before the Cleansing, and the new, correct books didn't hold quite the same sense of wonder or adventure.

By and by, Dion began to notice a golden glow to the edges of her book. It haloed the wrist and the hand that were holding the book aloft, a soft, magical luminosity that made her reach out to touch it with her other hand. It was ethereal but somehow heavy in the air. Dion caught a breath in her throat and dropped her book, her eyes flying at once to the man in the mirror. He was looking right at her, and on the mirror was an embossing in the same gold that formed curlicues up and down the glass. Dion, her mouth as wide open as her eyes, watched in fascination as the curlicues gained form and structure, and became words.

The words in the mirror said: *Don't they teach you about sound?*

"Sound is vibration," said Dion doubtfully, sitting up with difficulty. She wasn't unsure about what sound was: she was unsure why it mattered. She had been right at first: this *was* a test. "I haven't seen– that is, the magic is beautiful. How do you– do you mind telling me how you're doing that?" He waited so long to respond that she had flushed and added hurriedly: "I'm sorry! Of course, you can't hear me. How silly of me," before the golden curlicues reformed to add: *What does that tell you?*

"You c– *can* hear me!" said Dion foolishly.

The words in the mirror swirled apart and then together again. *I can read your lips. Face the mirror, please.*

Dion turned her head a little more. "Well, vibrations. You speak, which makes the air vibrate, and then those vibrations play against– oh! Oh, I know!"

The glass in the mirror was stopping the vibrations from coming through and getting to her ears. That's why he seemed not to make any sound though his mouth moved. Dion wriggled painfully toward the edge of her bed, a pale reflection of herself grimacing and haltingly stumbling forward in the mirror. The Fae, who somehow seemed more real than she did in that reflection, simply waited. Dion's ankle ached and throbbed, but she continued doggedly on until she could place her palm on the mirror. She wasn't yet proficient enough with magic to affect

5

things she wasn't touching, and she regretted it more than ever now.

The Fae waited for her without impatience. He didn't seem to be concerned with her pain, though Dion thought that he watched her very carefully, and when she at last laid her palm against the mirror, damp with sweat, he gave her a single, short nod. It said *well done*, though the mirror didn't.

Vibrations, thought Dion, and sent a tracery of raw magic into the mirror. In the mirror, the Fae spoke, and she felt the vibration of it against her vein-work of magic. The mirror was too thick to allow the vibrations through, and Dion was wary of softening it. Fae though he might be, she wasn't sure she wanted him stepping through the mirror along with his voice. She left her tracery of magic where it was, and opened up the thread that linked his side to hers into a small spider-web on her side of the mirror.

It wasn't until a deep, rough voice said: "Good technique," that Dion was sure it had worked. The curlicues disappeared, and for the first time she got a really good look at the Fae, unfestooned by gold or seen as a flicker in the corner of her eyes. He was very tall and broad in the shoulders, with a badly scarred face and a huge greatsword that was bigger than Dion. It occurred to her, belatedly, that despite the colour of his skin, he didn't at all look like a Fae. She'd thought of him as Fae by default, for what could an ordinary man be doing in her mirror, after all?

"Your magic is very strong," he said.

Dion, both embarrassed and hot with pain, said: "Thank you."

"Don't thank me," he said. "You'll regret it, in time."

Dion didn't like to contradict him, but she was quite certain she would always be glad for her skill in magic. Since that thought verged on rebellion, she quickly pushed it away and said: "Are you here to protect me?"

"Yes," he said. "And no."

"Are you here to teach me?"

"Yes. And no."

That was certainly very Fae-like. Dion, daring one more question, asked: "What will you teach me?"

"Two things," said the Fae. "How to use your magic. And how to die."

Perhaps the Fae saw her shivers. He said: "You're not going to die for a long while yet, Dion ferch Alawn. And when you do, it will be for your people."

"Oh," said Dion. She straightened her shoulders, though she didn't stop shivering. "That's different. That's all right."

The Fae studied her, frowning. "Is it?"

"Yes," Dion said, because it was true. But she did hope that when the time came to die she wouldn't feel so sick and weak. Aerwn had always been the brave, heroic one. "That's an honour."

"I'm Barric," he said.

Dion, who knew how unlike the Fae it was to offer a name at first meeting, was surprised. She made the Curtsey of High Respect that she had been taught to give the High Fae and pretended that it didn't hurt her ankle.

Barric took it expressionlessly and said: "We'll start with the base elements of raw magic. You'll need to get a book from the library."

Dion couldn't help the small, disappointed 'oh' that escaped her. She had been attentively studying magic for the last two years, and book spells were easy. It was the freeform *doing* of magic that she had hoped to be taught. Her Instructor of Magic was reluctant to depart from assigned spells, though Dion didn't know why.

It was difficult to say exactly how he did it, because he didn't actually smile, but Dion had the impression that Barric was amused. "Disappointed, Dion ferch Alawn?"

Politeness dictated that she should politely lie. Fae rules said that you didn't ever lie to the Fae. At length, in an agony of fear, she said: "Yes. Sorry."

He said: "It's not a spell book. Book magic is not the kind of knowledge you'll need."

"What kind of book is it?"

"Poetry," said Barric. Dion thought he might be laughing at her again—the Fae were fond of teasing her in small, cutting ways—but there wasn't a smile in his eyes as there had been before. *The Song of the Broken Sword.* Take it early in the morning and put it back before nightfall. Come to me again when you've memorised the second canto of the third song."

He disappeared without another word, and Dion was left to her thoughts and a painful struggle back to bed. The library was patrolled once in the morning and once at nightfall. Dion knew this, but she wondered how Barric did. If he was telling her to make sure the book was back before night patrol, *The Song of the Broken Sword* must be one of the Forbidden Books: illegal to read but too valuable to destroy. There were still a few of those, despite the Cleansing. *A Fae always has a reason for what that which he does. It is not for mortals to question or upbraid,* but Dion wasn't at all keen to break the law. Still, *Fae commands are to be obeyed absolutely. Though human eyes may not see to the conclusion, the winding path leads to the same end as the straight path.*

Thus it was, a week later, that Dion ferch Alawn committed her first act of deliberate law-breaking. She trembled all the way to the library, started at every curtsey and greeting along the way, and felt so sick once she arrived that she almost disgraced herself behind one of the padded reading benches. She collected a pile of books in which to hide her misdeeds, and then draped the fluffy morning shawl she had brought along around *that*, wending a carefully aimless path through the stacks to the back corner where all the Forbidden Books were housed. She was especially careful to keep out of sight of the Keeper of the Library, who had a bad habit of treading so silently across the boards that he could be behind a careless patron before they were aware of it. Fortunately, the only other person in the library was one of Dion's old tutors, the Duc Owain ap Rees. She had always liked Owain, with his wiry, red beard and fierce, bushy eyebrows, though he often frightened her with the sharp fierceness of his eyes. Dion inclined her head to him as he stood and bowed, felt his hard old eyes focus on her, and scuttled away again, taking the long way around to the Forbidden Section.

The Song of the Broken Sword was on the top shelf of the section. Dion, settling her pile of books on the floorboards and tucking her knit wrap back around herself, stared up at it in dismay. She couldn't drag one of the large book ladders around to the shelf: the Keeper would be sure to notice. Aerwn would have climbed the bookshelves without a second thought, but Dion had never been particularly good with heights, and she began the necessary climb with hands that were even damper than before. The shelves were quite slick with dust by the time she reached the higher shelves, and for every gritty, slippery hand-hold Dion gained, she felt a little sicker. When she was finally able to reach the top shelf, shivering and sticky with sweat, it was some time before she could bring herself to stretch out a hand to take the book. Clinging tight to the shelf with one hand and puffing dust into the air with her quick breaths, Dion used the other hand to tip the book from its place and frantically seized the shelf once again. Now what? The book was thin enough to slip beneath her chin, but Dion wasn't anxious to let go of the shelf again. She wasn't even sure she could relax the white-knuckled grip of her fingers enough to climb back down.

Dion took in a shaky breath, let go of the shelf once again, and made a frantic grab for *The Song of the Broken Sword*. There was the soft *swiiip!* of dust slipping beneath the fingers that still gripped the shelf, and then she was falling backwards. Dion had no time to cry out, no time to consider that when she hit the floor it would be impossible to hide her perfidy in all the clatter. Someone wiry caught her around the knees and neck as she fell, the book slapping against her face painfully before Dion caught it again. She found herself looking up at Duc Owain ap Rees, who looked back down at her from under beetled, orangey brows, reminding her irresistibly of a large, angry owl.

He hefted her into a more comfortable position and said: "That is a dangerous book to be playing with, Dion ferch Alawn."

Dion, her face white and stiff, said, "Um," but the Duc wasn't listening. He was already striding for the opposite end of the library, Dion still in his arms and *The Song of the Broken Sword* pressed between them where it had fallen. She thought for a terrified moment that he was taking her to the keeper of the library, but he swept her right out the library doors and didn't stop walking until they were in one of the upper smoking rooms. There he deposited Dion on a tobacco-scented footstool in front of the fire and stood back with the book in one hand and the other folded behind him as if he were preparing to lecture her.

"Do you know what this book is, princess?"

"Poetry," said Dion, clutching her fingers together through the holes in her knit wrap. Aerwn wouldn't have been caught. Aerwn would have slipped in and out like a ghost, eluding both the keeper and Owain ap Rees. Oh, wouldn't Barric be disappointed in her!

"There are only two copies of this book in existence," said Owain. "This one was very nearly destroyed in the Cleansing. Do you know why?"

Hesitantly, Dion suggested: "It has sub– subversive themes?"

Owain gave a tough old grin beneath his beard. "You could say that. It's a special kind of poetry."

Dion felt a little fizz of excitement in her stomach. "It's *prophecy?*"

"Not all of it," said Owain ap Rees, flipping pages with his thumb. Even before he found the place and opened the book properly, Dion was quite sure where he would open it. Sure enough, one gnarled finger tapped a page on which the second canto of the third song began. "The Avernsian enchantresses wrote this many years ago."

"What is it about?"

"A fabled broken sword: a relic from the days when Faery and the human world were kept safe from each other. It was said that its forging combined the strongest of Fae and human magic, and that its guarding power was what kept Faery from overgrowing its bounds and taking over the human world as well."

"How did it break?"

"According to legend, it was believed that pieces of a broken sword would be safer and easier to hide." The Duc's moustache bristled with irritation, and he added with something of a snap: "None of our ancestors seem to have thought that a broken sword would lose something of its power in the breaking, and even as the Broken Sword began to fade from history to legend, its power was discovered to be less than hoped. Doors were forced open. Rifts were torn."

"–and the Guardians began to rise against the Fae," Dion said, eager to show her knowledge. She had been well-taught in Faery History.

Duc Owain ap Rees stared at her in silence for a moment, his brows lowered. At last he said: "Hfm. Well, perhaps it's best not to rail on the stupidity of our ancestors. We've enough of our own mistakes to lament."

Dion hunched her shoulders a little against the Duc's fierce eyebrows, unsure of his meaning and not quite sure if he were angry at her or the Llassarians of time past. She asked: "May I read the book?"

"Of course, Dion ferch Ywain," said Owain, giving Dion her ancestral name. She looked at him wonderingly and took the book. Her ancestral name was not often mentioned, and she always had the feeling that her parents were ashamed of it. Ywain had been a great persecutor of the Fae. "Read. It's your right."

Dion looked down, made uncomfortable by the Duc's steady regard, and read the second canto of the third song.

. . .

THEN THE BORDERS *shall rend*
  And darkness shall rise
  Stealing heat from the sun
  And light from the skies.

YET YWAIN'S YOUNG *daughter*
  And Coinneach's son
  In forging and binding
  the sword shall be one.

THE LOST SHALL BE FOUND,
  The broken rebound.

THEN DOES *Coinneach's son*
  The broken remake
  His hammer and anvil
  Consumed for its sake;

AND YWAIN'S YOUNG DAUGHTER,
  Sword in her hand, gives
  her life in the binding
  To seal up the land.

THE FORGING MADE *new*
  Unbroken and true.

SO THIS WAS what Barric had meant. She was Ywain's daughter—
many, many generations back—and this was how she was to die.

Saving the people of two worlds. The thought was less shivery than it had been last week.

"Isn't it lucky there are two of us?" she said, speaking her thoughts aloud.

Owain's eyebrows shot up and lowered again. "Do you understand what this means?"

Dion nodded. "When I am queen I will die for my people," she said. "But Aerwn will be queen after me, so it's all right."

There was a moment of silence. Then Owain ap Rees dropped to one knee as he had when he was first presented to Dion, and, taking her hand in his, he kissed it. It was homage due to a queen, not a Princess Heir sitting cross-legged on a footstool with a book in her lap.

"It's all right," Dion said again, leaning forward to put her other hand on Owain's shoulder. "Aerwn will be a better queen, anyway."

The Duc harrumphed and stood again with a slightly arthritic lurch. "Perhaps. You'd better give that to me when you're finished with it. You've run enough risk for one day: I'll take it back to the library after lunch."

"*Thank* you!" said Dion gladly, her heart buoying up again. She had not been looking forward to going back into the library.

When Barric appeared that night Dion was already waiting for him, her legs crossed and her elbows on her knees, attention brightly fixed on the mirror. Barric took her in, his dark eyes flicking from her toes—curled to stop them from wriggling—to her rumpled curls—a mop that had been pushed so often out of her eyes that it was slightly sideways—and she saw the scars on the right side of his face twitch slightly. From Barric, that was tantamount to a chuckle. Dion didn't mind Barric laughing at her. It never had the sting she felt from the amused, glittering eyes of her Fae maids.

"I s-stole it!" she said breathlessly, but she couldn't help the way her eyes flickered nervously around the room. Barric's scars moved again, and the faint suggestion of lines appeared by his eyes. Dion, aware that she had been indecorously loud, added self-consciously: "I memorised it and it's back in the library, just like you wanted."

Barric folded his arms and said: "Repeat it."

Dion said it back to him with barely a halting word. She loved to be certain and sure of her way, and as dreadful as it was, the certainty of her death when she was queen was almost a comfort. When she was finished Barric gave her a short, slow nod: it meant *well done*, Dion knew, and she flushed with pleasure.

He asked: "Did you read the rest of it?"

"A little bit of it," she said uncomfortably. Barric didn't look angry, but the rest of *The Song of the Broken Sword* had been less than complimentary to the Fae, and Dion had skipped over large portions of it with a rather scared look around. It was no wonder the book was on the Forbidden shelf. "I read the bit where they used the Broken Sword to seal up the border between Faery and our world. Is that what I have to do?"

It made sense: the Fae fled from the Guardians in their own lands, and by all accounts the Guardians were not a people that would stop at murdering humans as well. If Dion could seal up the border between the two once all the fleeing Fae were safe in the human world, it would save not only the Fae, but the human kingdoms as well.

"When the time comes," nodded Barric. "It won't be easy: the shards are spread across the human kingdoms, and you'll need to find them first."

"They should have kept them together," said Dion wisely.

Barric's dark eyes were amused. "They're safer apart until the Sword can be reforged. Not everyone has your high ideals, Dion ferch Ywain. There are many ways in which the shards can and have been misused."

"But when will I know it's time? If people are being hurt *now—*"

"You'll know the time when it comes," said Barric gently. "You've much to learn before you can hope to seal up the land. Don't be so eager to die for nothing."

DION WAS APPOINTED a new tutor when she turned eight. It came as a surprise to her, surrounded as she was by history tutors, policy advisors, dancing teachers, and civic responsibility instructors. This tutor was Fae like the rest of them, but there the similarities ended. Where her other tutors were cold but reasonably respectful, Tutor Iceflame was cruel, cutting, and entirely merciless. Her purpose seemed to be to teach Dion to look cool and aloof even when she wasn't cool and aloof. Unfortunately for Dion, she blushed when she was embarrassed, stumbled over her tongue when she was nervous, and hunched her shoulders inward when she wished to be unnoticed. Tutor Iceflame noticed all of this, and took swift, merciless steps to ensure that it was corrected. Dion learned a series of carefully constructed expressions that she practised into front of her mirror under Tutor Iceflame's cold, narrow gaze, while the tutor snapped questions, insults, and instructions. Her shoulders were bound to a wooden frame that chafed her skin and forced her to stand with her shoulders back, her chin high and graceful. In time she became used to the insults and questions that Iceflame threw at her, and no longer blushed at either. It was more difficult in everyday life, where Dion was never quite sure what to prepare for, but with Iceflame it was possible to arrange herself mentally and put on the right expressions. And so long as Dion was ready for Iceflame every day, she was reasonably certain that nothing worse could happen. She learned to use faces #1-5 for varying degrees of polite interest (and interest was *never* to appear anything more than polite), faces #6-11 for differing levels of polite surprise, and #12-50 for a range of other approved emotions. She grew weary of her own face in the mirror as it segued between false emotions, but when Tutor Iceflame swept out of the room every day, her glimmering train of satin flying behind her, there was always Barric. Barric with his blessed silence and almost mono-syllaballic commands as he taught her the very warp and weft of magic. Barric and his harsh, scarred face that belied his kind eyes. Barric teaching her how to clean a sword. Barric making caustic remarks about Tutor Iceflame. Most of all, Barric listening to Dion's short, muddled, and unhappy woes. He didn't become impatient with her like Aerwn did, nor did he mock her fears and sense of duty. He simply listened. And by the time Dion muddled to the end of her troubles, she always knew it wasn't as bad as it had seemed before. It was Barric she went to when Aerwn first started sneaking out of the castle, Barric who taught her the steps to the latest impossible Faery dance by teaching her several opening footwork gambits of Faery swordplay, Barric who listened when Dion's first sweetheart preferred Aerwn to Dion.

Dion's Faery tutors pinched, pulled, ordered, sniffed, and sighed. They were—understandably, Dion knew—impatient and sharp with her shortcomings. They were moulding a queen, and what else was to be expected? But Barric was never short, had a comforting way of saying nothing at all, and occasionally even smiled. Dion grew to love his huge silence.

THE YEAR DION TURNED ELEVEN, she accidentally let slip that she often talked with a man in her bedroom. It caused a furore in the breakfast room that startled Dion by exploding through the whole castle as guards, magicians, and Fae were sent running to her suite. Dion was kept by the frightened king and queen in the breakfast room until her room was declared to be entirely free of enchantments and men alike. Nevertheless, the king and queen murmured worriedly back and forth out of hearing of the twins at one end of the room. The Fae were less worried. The tutors, their eyes dark and glittering, questioned Dion, and at last pronounced the conclusion that the intruder was a Fae. High Fae, they said, their eyes glittering all the more when they learned that Barric's skin was as dark as the rich soil of Llassar. A prince in Faery, no doubt: only the Highest of Fae could broach the barrier between the Human World and Faery without help. And only the Highest of Fae had skin of any other colour than the usual, translucent, moonlight white.

Dion didn't contradict it, but she was quite sure by now that Barric wasn't Fae. He was too big and solid, and his face was too honestly harsh. The Fae were much more ethereal in their good looks. Besides, Barric had a long, ragged scar that ran across his face from below his left eye and across his nose to pull up the right side of his mouth. None of the Fae Dion knew could bear to leave their faces so: the Fae had a horror of mutilation. But she didn't tell her questioners any of that, nor did she mention the prophecy or her fated death. She didn't want to sadden her parents. More importantly, she was aware in a deep, certain kind of way that it was something not to be spoken of, even to the Fae or her parents.

The King and Queen were at last satisfied by the Fae: and why wouldn't they be? It was an honour for Dion to be so singled out by the High Fae. But Dion noticed that Aerwn, who had grown slightly quieter as she grew older, stared at her with a slight frown between her eyebrows. Aerwn obviously didn't think it was an honour. Dion herself was merely glad to have the fuss over and done with.

THE YEAR that Dion and Aerwn turned thirteen was a lonely one for Dion. She and Barric quarrelled badly and unexpectedly at the start of the year, and she didn't speak with him for most of the year. Dion had always known that *The Song of the Broken Sword* was forbidden and probably treasonous, but although she was certain Barric was no Fae, it had still come as a shock when he began to insinuate, carefully and gently, that the Fae had come to Llassar with overthrow in their minds. Dion had at first felt uncomfortable, and then repulsed. Finally, when Barric went on to point out, even more carefully and gently, her parents' part in the overthrow, she had become very angry.

Her painstakingly learned expressions forgotten in a flush of anger, Dion stood abruptly and said: "You're a l-liar! You won't say those things about my parents! I w-won't listen!" She had heard him calling after her, and she still saw him briefly every now and then—even heard a word or two before she hurried away—but she had never stayed for long enough to be sure.

Labouring under Tutor Iceflame's instructions without even the quiet comfort of Barric's companionship afterwards was gruelling work, and Dion saw her own face reflected hollowly back at her as she practised in the mirror, growing thinner and more solemn as the year progressed. Despite that, she made sure that she was away from the mirror when Iceflame left. She didn't want to run the risk of seeing Barric again. She had the feeling that she would forgive him if he asked her to, and she didn't think it was right to do so.

Adding to Dion's loneliness was the fact that Aerwn was gone for most of the year. She had begun it by running away from the castle and had been caught trying to sneak out of Harlech at the changing of the watch that night. Why she would do such a thing puzzled Dion exceedingly, but she wasn't given the chance to ask her sister about it. The King and Queen sent Aerwn away quickly and quietly, though Dion was never told where.

"Somewhere quiet," said the Queen, when Dion finally got up the courage to ask. "She needs peace and quiet, darling. Her mind is disordered. She always was inclined to be excited, and the Fae know what they're doing."

Wherever it was that she went, Aerwn was gone for the better part of ten months, and when she came back Dion found that her sister wasn't quite *there*, exactly. Not right away. Their parents wouldn't allow Dion to see Aerwn alone, and when she saw her sister at meals, Aerwn was pale and silent, refusing to look anyone in the eye. She wouldn't respond to conversation, and after a little while Dion stopped trying to talk to her.

At last, when it seemed that Aerwn was never to emerge from her suite unaccompanied by two Fae maids, and that Dion was never to be allowed in to see her, Dion took matters into her own hands. Perhaps it was the corrupting result of book-stealing that made her so willing to consider disobedience. Perhaps it was simply Aerwn's shuttered eyes, which had once been so bright and open. Whatever the reason, Dion rose from her bed one morning and methodically made a back door through to her sister's suite. It was a simple enough matter: their bathing chambers shared a common wall, through which Dion sometimes heard faint noises when Aerwn was being particularly difficult. The practical magic she had been learning from Barric had been so well absorbed that it was the work of only a few minutes to convince part of the wall that it wasn't quite solid, and to construct a doorway to hold up the rest of the wall around the weakened part. Dion, moving carefully through the softened part of the wall, found herself in Aerwn's ablutions chamber without feeling that she had done something so very unusual.

Aerwn was sitting in her window when Dion stole softly into the main room of her suite. Aerwn's feet were bare and she was dressed only in a shift, her side pressed against the glass and her eyes unfocused on the vista below.

"You'll get sick," Dion said, fetching her sister's slippers.

Aerwn's head jerked around in swift, sharp fright, her feet shifting beneath her in a moment. She looked ready to leap for Dion's throat. Then a flash of recognition came to her eyes, and they brightened in the first sign of real emotion Dion had seen from her sister in the month since she'd returned home.

"You shouldn't be in here," Aerwn said, tugging on her slippers. "I'm delicate, didn't you hear?"

"Delicate," said Dion. "Is that what it is?"

"No," said Aerwn, and Dion wasn't quite sure whether she was serious or laughing. "I'm addled. You can see it in the whites of my eyes. They've magicked my windows, Di."

Dion glanced at the windows, but they were simply glass and filigree. She didn't like to tell Aerwn that, because it was this kind of talk that had led to Aerwn being sent away in the first place, and she wasn't quite sure that Aerwn was looking well again, despite her smile.

Aerwn slipped down from the window-embrasure, her feet light on the carpet, and clutched at Dion's hand. "You see it, don't you, Di? I can't open 'em. They've magicked 'em shut so that I can't get out."

"I can't see anything," Dion said reluctantly. She was beginning to think this visit was a rather bad mistake. "There's nothing there, Aerwn."

Her sister looked at her narrowly for a few charged moments, and then, to Dion's relief, nodded. "All right," she said. "If you say so, I believe you. You're the one with magic, and you wouldn't lie to me."

Dion let out a tiny breath of relief. "I missed you," she said. "You've been gone for so long."

"I think I missed you," said Aerwn, her eyes losing focus. "Things got a bit cloudy for a while in the middle, but I remember thinking about you. Dee, I can't get out of the windows. They're still playing tricks on me. Maybe it's me. Did they put a spell on me?"

Dion started to say "There isn't a spell on you", but stopped. There *was* a spell on Aerwn. It was clinging and beautiful and almost invisible. It looked a little like the misdirection magic that Barric had taught her. She said: "Show me. Try to open the window."

Aerwn, her eyes blessedly attentive again, tried to open the window. Somehow her hands managed to slide past the latch every time she tried to turn it, and even when Dion turned it for her, she couldn't manage to press her hands against the glass to shove it open.

Dion, who had been watching with a deep furrow between her brows, said: "Who did this to you?"

Aerwn shrugged. "Any one of 'em could have done it. They like playing with me. For all I know, it could have been one of the maids."

"We should tell Mother and Father," said Dion, a shaking anger growing in her. "Have both of your maids dismissed."

Aerwn grew pale. "No!"

"But if–"

"I said no!" Dion took a step back, feeling slapped, and her sister said gruffly: "You don't understand, Dee. They'll just send someone worse."

"Who is *they*?" demanded Dion in despair. It was so like Aerwn to inflate a nasty joke into something frightening and fictitious.

"Never mind," said Aerwn, her eyes once more shuttered. "Can you get it off me?"

Dion struggled with words that wouldn't come, and finally said: "Yes. Yes, all right." She studied the enchantment in all its clever, glittering beauty, her fingers curled in the soft weaving of her morning wrap. It didn't seem to have a beginning or an end, almost as if someone had made a fine diamond-net and thrown it over Aerwn in passing. Dion lifted it carefully, wary of the sharp diamond edges, and threw it fastidiously into one corner of Aerwn's suite when it had cleared her sister's head. It glittered there for a moment and then seemed to melt away. Aerwn, aware from Dion's tossing motion that she was free, immediately turned back to the window and opened it. When the breeze sneaked in, cool and wet, she smiled. Dion felt rather sadly that she'd been forgotten, but then Aerwn put her back to the window to smile at her. It was a real, lively, familiar smile.

"Well now!" she said. "I feel much better!"

"If someone is playing tricks on you, you really should mention it to Mother and Father," said Dion, willing to give it one more chance. Aerwn always did as she pleased, of course, but it couldn't hurt to try again.

"Never mind that now," said Aerwn. "I'll just have to be more careful. You've been learning more magic, haven't you? Is your imaginary friend still visiting you?"

"Not more, just different," said Dion, and added uncomfortably: "He's not imaginary."

"*I've* never seen him," Aerwn said, her eyes dancing. She was becoming swiftly more like the Aerwn that Dion had grown up with. Dion wondered exactly what else there had been in that spell, and regretted that she couldn't now examine it properly. "Just who *has* seen him, I'd like to know? Apart from you? And they say *I'm* crackers!"

Dion couldn't help laughing. "No one says you're crackers!"

"Not in so many words," said Aerwn cheerfully. "No, they're cleverer than that. Just a little word here and there and off you go to have your head fixed. Oh, don't get that disapproving look, Dee; I'll be good. Look, if you've been practising your magic, d'you think you can make me a handy little spell?"

"What sort of spell?" Dion said cautiously. She knew Aerwn too well.

"Nothing naughty," said Aerwn. "Do you remember those fighters we saw when we were four? The ones they rubbed down with oil so that they could barely grapple?"

Dion chewed her bottom lip, her thoughts turning and sparking. "I can make a spell like that. It'll take a few days."

"All right," Aerwn said. "Oh b– I mean bother! That's the maids at the door: if you stay here they'll tell Mother. I suppose you can get back in again when the spell's done?"

Dion nodded.

"All right. Don't forget about it," said Aerwn. She hugged Dion briefly, and Dion felt her tremble slightly as she said: "Thanks, Dee."

It would have been easier to make the spell that Aerwn wanted if she could discuss it with Barric, Dion knew. She didn't want to admit it to herself, but she very much missed him—had done so since her anger had died the first day—and it was only by remembering the things Barric had said about her parents that she held firm to her conviction and avoided her mirror. She wouldn't be friends with someone who spoke of her parents in such a manner. She wouldn't ask such a person for help with a spell, and she certainly wouldn't keep looking over at her mirror and wondering why she hadn't seen scrap nor shadow of Barric in it for the last few days. He had been trying to catch her attention for months now, and though Dion was quite determined that she wasn't going to associate with him any longer, she felt somehow abandoned; as if Barric and not she had been the one to break things off.

Dion pushed away the thought and went back to her spell. It was useless to think about Barric, and worse than useless to miss him. She would create the spell by herself, and then she would attend her lessons like a proper heir: living as well as she could until the time came to die. Surely if she kept practising, she would be prepared when the time came to reforge the Broken Sword. If only there hadn't been a fire in the library last year! Dion would have liked to read the whole of *The Song of the Broken Sword*, not just the bits and pieces around second canto of the third song. Beyond the certainty that there were seven shards to gather and the almost-certainty that the Binding would need to take place in Avernse where the original Binding had happened, there was still a great deal she didn't know about the Broken Sword. Dion found, amongst all her regrets, one that Avernse and Llassar were not on better terms: the king would never allow her to make a visit to Avernse. There was no chance that Dion would ever be able to study the only remaining copy of *The Song of the*

Broken Sword in existence. If Avernse had been willing to succour the Fae, there would have been no impediment. Unfortunately, she couldn't even visit Montalier, which was rumoured to have strong ties to Avernse, because the Montalierans had also refused to help the Fae by so much as a house in which to stay. Alawn ap Fane had waxed loud and eloquent in his disapprobation of both countries. No, Dion was on her own.

The next day, Dion took herself to the gardens. While Aerwn took to the exciting and forbidden streets of Harlech to sate her dissatisfaction with life, Dion found peace and solace in the castle gardens. No one but royalty was allowed in the copses and carefully maintained hedges between the hours of noon and early tea, and when Dion was feeling particularly put upon she tended to escape into the quiet greenery. It was the only place she could depend upon being thoroughly alone: even the Fae didn't visit the gardens. In fact, unusually enough for a people who loved nature in all its forms, they avoided them assiduously even in the allowed hours. The gardens, in fact, were a lot like Barric: large and quiet and peaceful.

"No!" said Dion aloud, startling herself. Here she was thinking of Barric again! And her carefully constructed spell *still* wouldn't work! She simply had to try harder.

A shadow fell over her, cool and sudden, and Dion sprang from her stone seat in some confusion. But when she turned to see who had approached her, it wasn't, as she had expected, either her mother or her father. It was Barric. Barric in flesh and blood, and far bigger than she'd ever realised. In person, she could fairly feel the power of his magic, distinctly unfamiliar. It wasn't Fae, but neither did it seem quite human.

Dion, her eyes wide and startled, automatically offered her hand, and with one knee to the ground Barric lowered his forehead to her fingers in the old manner– a supplicant seeking pardon.

"Oh, don't!" she protested.

Barric didn't move, didn't so much as raise his head. He said: "Forgive me."

"Oh no, no, no!" said Dion, and threw her arms around his neck. *"Don't,* Barric! What are you doing here? How are you here? I'm sorry– I'm so sorry– but–"

Barric picked her up and hugged her in return. Being hugged by Barric was like being lightly crushed in a large, warm vice. Dion had the feeling that he was trying to be careful not to break her. She said, for the second time in as many days: "I missed you."

Barric put her back down, his big hands covering each of her arms from elbow to shoulder. "I can stay only briefly," he said, and there was an urgency in his eyes that made Dion feel ashamed of herself. "There is too much to learn and too little time. We won't speak of your parents again, but we must continue."

"I will," Dion promised. "I mean, yes, we'll keep going. I'm sorry– but no, I'm not–"

Barric nodded, with a slight upward pull of his scar. "I understand."

"You don't know them," said Dion, tumbling into speech. "You don't, Barric, or you wouldn't think– you *couldn't* think–"

"Peace," said Barric. "I've promised. I won't speak of them."

There was nothing to be dissatisfied about in that, but Dion found herself looking rather searchingly at him. Barric seemed to notice, and though his scar jumped a little he said quietly: "Trust me?"

"I do," Dion said: and she did, so what was there to worry her?

LIFE WAS PLEASANTER with Barric in it again. And when Barric *wasn't* there, Aerwn was: lovable, mad, and unexpected. She disrupted Dion's state lessons and made faces at her when Dion was trying to look interested in what visiting princes and dignitaries thought about the rate of exchange between Llassarian pennies and Illisrian drachs. She had accepted the spell that Dion finally crafted with a wholly speculative gleam to her eye that made Dion wonder exactly why she wanted a spell that would slough off all other magic, and refused to speak any more about it. When Dion tried to make Aerwn be serious, Aerwn joked her out of her seriousness. She told dreadful stories, and Dion could never be quite certain if she was lying or not, because Aerwn had the most solemn face when she was spouting the most ridiculous nonsense. And as they grew older Aerwn's habit of saying odd, uncomfortable things and making suggestions that made no sense to the more honest Dion grew even more prevalent. It was perhaps because of these differences rather than in spite of them that the two sisters only drew closer as they grew older. There was no one else like Aerwn.

It didn't really occur to Dion until she was fifteen that there was a difference between Aerwn when she was with Dion and Aerwn when she was with their parents. It was just another facet of Aerwn's slightly duplicitous nature, that need to play a part or make fun of whomever she was with. It wasn't until the night that Aerwn climbed in through Dion's bedroom window bleeding and bruised, with a look in her eyes that Dion didn't understand, that she saw the difference. Aerwn had always sneaked out of the castle and into Harlech—it was one of her princessly rebellions—but she had never come home bleeding before. She wouldn't let Dion call a Fae maid or do anything except heal the sluggishly bleeding wound. Her blood-soaked clothes and pale face suggested that she had already bled quite significantly, and by the time Dion had healed the wound with shaking fingers, Aerwn was half-fainting, half-sleeping on Dion's bed. Confused, worried, and frightened, Dion had curled under the covers with her sister as if they were three again, and woke in the morning to find Aerwn already gone.

Aerwn was perfectly cheerful and inclined to be dismissive with Dion anxiously sought her out the next day, laughing away her sister's fears and questions. When Dion went to her parents with the worried suspicion that Aerwn was getting into dangerous scrapes, she found that her parents were very well aware her sister still often slipped out of the castle.

"It's nothing to worry about, dear one," said her mother. "I was wild enough myself as a child. A second princess has nothing else to occupy her time but making mischief, and so long as she takes a Fae maid with her, she can't be otherwise than safe."

"She was *bleeding*, Mother."

King Alawn ap Fane smiled at Dion indulgently. "She told us she'd frightened you with some prank or other, perilous child that she is! You know how she is, Dion: any mischief for a laugh. Don't worry your mind about it. She'll calm when she marries."

Dion, who was absolutely certain that Aerwn had not been counterfeiting either injury or faint, tried to convince them otherwise, but her parents were not inclined to believe her. And the next time they sat together as a family she watched Aerwn more critically, not as a fond sister but as an impartial observer. Where Aerwn with Dion was laughing but sometimes sombre, Aerwn with her parents was always bright, always laughing; while with Dion she was clever and even sometimes thoughtful, when with her parents, Aerwn was always bubbling and never deep enough to have a real conversation. With Dion she talked frowningly of unrest in Illisr and skirmishes in Montalier. With her parents she mouthed frothy popular opinions and made fun of the staid old politicians of the old, pre-Fae days.

It occurred to Dion for the first time that Aerwn was playing a game, wearing a laughing, silly mask, and that if she was not being honest with her parents, neither was she being quite honest with Dion. It made her even more cautious about believing everything Aerwn said, and though she didn't begin to love her sister any less, she did feel that some distance had been made between the two of them– and that the distance wasn't of her own making.

2

THE FIRST CHILL OF AUTUMN

*I*t was late afternoon, and an unusually bright piece of sunshine had filtered through the clouds to play on Dion's bedspread. Summer in Llassar, as Aerwn said, simply meant that there was a little sunshine in the rain. That the sunshine had stretched out just a little longer each day over the last ten years or so was seen as a happy coincidence with the high population of Seelie Fae who had made Llassar their home.

Aerwn, like the sunshine, was at present stretched out on top of Dion's bed. Unlike the sunshine, she was a lively, unsettling presence. Her tall, lissom figure was thrown out at ease and perfectly relaxed but her speech fluttered here and there with baffling logic. So like and yet unlike Dion, her hair was just as black and curling, but where Dion's hair was kept long Aerwn had many years since rebelled by cutting hers short in a mop of curls. The biggest difference, thought Dion, as she changed out of morning dress between two court sessions, was the fiery, fierce, energetic *life* to Aerwn. Beside her, Dion was cold, stupid, and silent; too afraid of showing more feeling than she ought, to show as much as she should, and too careful of her expressions to touch anyone with real warmth of feeling. Aerwn may have her faults in too hasty speech and impatience, but she was more alive than Dion.

Dion twisted her mouth in dissatisfaction as she smoothed her skirts straight, and swept over to her dressing mirror.

"You know, you're the only girl I know who doesn't dress in *front* of her mirror," said Aerwn. She was tossing grapes in the air and catching them with her mouth.

"Aren't you supposed to be with your tutor?" countered Dion, a little flustered by the sudden attack. The twins had had their seventeenth birthday a few days ago, and although it made scant difference to Aerwn, it had meant a great deal more work for Dion. Her Court sessions were for the purpose of honorifically declaring her as the heir of Llassar, and tomorrow the coronal tour around Llassar would begin. She had been the Princess Heir since birth, but today her adult status and Heirship were to be ceremonially declared. There was a great deal to do and prepare for. "I'm sure you're meant to be with your tutor."

"We had a difference of opinion."

"Oh, Aerwn, not again!"

"I don't particularly like being lied to. He's a silver-tongued little twerp who thinks he's a lot more important than he is."

Dion huffed a little sigh and tried not to let it ruin the line of her shoulders. She needed her shoulders loose for face #51— regal attentiveness—which would be her default expression for the next few days. "Mother is going to be annoyed that you've left early again."

"I think it's his sense of entitlement that irks me the most, though," pursued Aerwn. "He positively *reeks* of it! I can see him looking down his beautifully narrow nose at me. Now, I'm no snob, Di, but if anyone should be looking down on anyone, it's *me*!"

Dion noticed the furrowed brow of her reflection and hastily smoothed it. "Aerwn, you're always saying people are lying to you. Mother is talking about having you seen to by Doctor Whishte. She's worried."

"Oh, they've already tried that," said Aerwn, her face suddenly as white as her shirt-sleeves. "It didn't *take*. And I'm always saying people are lying to me because they are. I should have been more careful at first. Now they lie to me just for fun, about stupid little things."

Dion took in another silent sigh. "Why do you always think people are lying to you?"

"If it comes to that, why do you always think everyone is telling you the truth?" said Aerwn. "You're so horribly honest, Di! I know it's hard to believe, but people lie. Humans lie. The Fae lie. Even Mother and Father lie."

"They don't– why– *who* do you think they're lying to?"

Aerwn's mouth, so similar to Dion's, quirked downwards. "Themselves, mostly. But to us, too."

"I don't have time to talk about this now," said Dion.

"Of course you don't," said her sister. She flicked her feet over the end of the bed and stood in one quick, angry motion. "And you're off around the country tomorrow, so there won't be any time to talk about it later, either. I suppose I'd better leave you to it. I wouldn't want to make you late."

"*Aerwn*," said Dion hopelessly.

From the door, her sister said: "While you're bouncing about the countryside in a fat Crown coach, try to remember what it was like before the Fae. Also, I love you."

TWO WEEKS LATER, Dion was heartily cursing her fat Crown coach. It was big and warm, and far too wide for the narrow Llassarian country roads that it had to travel. The front axle, taking exception to one too many ditches in conjunction with one too many lumps in the road, had splintered and broken as they rounded the latest corner. The axles would once have been iron and far less likely to break, but now that the Fae were so prevalent in Llassar metallurgy was generally frowned upon and only barely legal. The Fae didn't care for iron. They didn't care much for any type of metal, as a matter of fact.

Dion, tossed forward into the lap of her personal maid, heard the shattering of one of the inner glass lanterns as the coach ground to a halt, and tried to pull herself back into her seat with as much dignity as she could muster. Oddly enough, none of the other four people in the coach attempted to help her. It wasn't until Dion was once again perched perilously upon her tilting seat that she realised why. All of them were asleep or unconscious, their heads drooping against their chests and their limbs loose and lax.

Her guards were at the coach doors on either side in a moment. "Your highness, are you injured?"

"D-don't open the doors!" Dion cried, her tongue tripping over the words in her haste; but she was too late. The doors opened together; and together, her two outer guards slumped forward until they were half in and half out of the coach.

Dion tumbled out of the coach over the prone bodies of her guards, quick and breathless, and ran for the first cover she could find with her skirts bunched around her knees. That first cover was a shallow ditch covered by the fine, drooping foliage of a feather-willow. She rolled into it, her heart beating hard in her ears, and waited for the ambush to descend upon her coach.

It never came. Crouched in a trembling heap with roots digging into her knees and palms, Dion quietly threw up on the grass. Then, when she was feeling well enough to force back her anxiety, she began to gather herself into some semblance of capable thinking. Something in the coach had set her retinue to sleep: the broken lantern, she guessed. It wasn't magical in origin, or both she and the Fae would have noticed. It had seemed logical that an attack would occur once they were all asleep. The question was, thought Dion, mechanically rubbing her palms up and down her forearms to try and rid herself of the trembling, why *hadn't* it happened? And why hadn't she fallen asleep as well? She set a quick trace of magic rippling over her body, but found nothing amiss that she could recognise.

Dion left her shelter and approached the coach again cautiously, trailing grass and dirt. Her travel wrap was wafting on the cool breeze, one corner of it caught in the hinge of the door. It must have wedged there when she leapt from the coach. It was threaded through with a rather carefully designed spell of her own making: when wrapped around her face during travel, it filtered out dust, unpleasant odours, and most chemicals that could be used to overcome an unwary human. Fae, who were largely unaffected by chemicals that rendered humans uncon-scious, had hitherto refused her offers of spelled equipment. After this trip, Dion was rather certain that she wouldn't have to insist.

She reached out to catch the end of her wrap. Had it been up when the accident happened? She thought it had been. Now that she wasn't feeling too ill to concentrate, she detected a certain soreness to her neck. She must have half-strangled herself when she left the coach.

Dion examined the thin weave a little more closely, and found that the filtering spell had been completely burned out. Not only that, the weave itself had bubbled in tiny, melted patches of fabric. Whatever had set her retinue to sleep, it was certainly airborne: it had completely burned out the spell.

More carefully now, Dion went on to examine her retinue. Medicinal magic wasn't a branch of magic that she had much studied: it required a knowledge of the human body, inside and out, that she simply hadn't had time to gain. More worryingly, her magic was coming up against something distinctly *metallic* in each member of her retinue's chests. Still, they didn't seem to be in danger of dying, merely sleeping for rather a long time. If she were to go for help, it was unlikely that they would worsen in the mean-time.

Dion took some time to shift the coach from the road to the cover of the willows. It took more than a little magical effort, but a royal coach would likely attract some attention, and not all of it pleasant. Someone, and for some reason, had already attacked. Until she could return with help, it seemed sensible to keep it out of sight. The horses, she took further from the road, following the line of willows until she found water. She left them with a slight suggestion of magic that would disincline them to wander from the stream, and went to the coach.

Her retinue and the horses taken care of, the first order of the day was to make herself look less princessly. Dion shut the Heir's Circlet of State in the carriage's lockbox, hoping the magics that protected it would be enough; but there was still the matter of her ridiculously long black curls and rather ostentatious over-dress with its royal insignia. Her height she could do nothing about, but the rest could be hidden. Dion had a wild, almost exited urge to cut off her hair, but she thought better of it very quickly. Mother and Father would be appalled; besides, it was the easiest thing in the world to plait it in one great rope down her back. She could cover the whole with her plainest scarf by passing it over her head and wrapping it around the plait at the back. She'd seen some of the girls in Bithywis—the last town they had visited—doing the same. Her overdress would have to come off, of course: she had a neat, warm jerkin and underskirt beneath, and even if her full sleeves where white muslin, it was unlikely they'd remain white for long in the dusty road. By the time she was done, Dion thought rather hopefully that she might pass muster as one of the town girls. She would have to be careful not to speak too much. Bithywis was close enough to Harlech to have much the same speech patterns, but there was still some-thing of the countrified air to the local speech that she would have trouble emulating.

I'll just have to mumble, she thought, with a tiny smile. Tutor Iceflame had spent many harsh hours with Dion, trying to break her of that very habit. Perhaps it would come in handy here in Bithywis. At any rate, it would be much wiser to pretend as far as possible until she could find someone official enough to present with her Royal Seal. Help would come swiftly enough after that.

She followed the road back for some way—further, in fact, than she thought they had come—and it was getting on for evening by the time she saw the wall of Bithywis again. It was a welcome sight: she felt imperilled and exposed on the road where anyone could see her. Aerwn wouldn't have been afraid, Dion thought uncomfortably; but she couldn't help the skittering feeling that *would* run up and down her neck every time she heard horse-hooves or footsteps turn onto the King's highway behind her. None of the other travellers seemed similarly troubled; they walked quickly and overtook Dion easily, their eyes on the road before them. At first she smiled shyly at them, but when none of them acknowledged her by so much as the flicker of an eyelash she began to feel that she was making herself noticeable, and turned her own eyes to the road. She did notice, however, that no matter how dissimilar the travellers were, each of them had a length of decorative chain about their necks, from which hung one of two types of disc: silver or copper. The only travellers who didn't have such discs, in fact, were Fae travellers. Was it some sort of fad? wondered Dion. If so, it was not a particularly fetching one.

Dion approached the main gates of Bithywis at much the same time as a wagon and a few other travellers. Her fellow travellers showed their discs and were allowed through, which prompted a slight panic of knowledge within Dion: they were identification chips, no doubt. Whatever the reason Bithywis' officials had thought it necessary to demand identification upon entry, it didn't matter: Dion had none.

She had stopped just outside the gate, lurking behind the

wagon and conveniently out of sight of the two guards to think it through—should she push on, or try to brazen it out?—when a musical but masculine voice said: "You're perturbed, sweeting."

Fae, Dion knew, even before turning. He was a froth of sable and diamond Faery magic behind her. What she didn't expect was for him to be wearing a guard's uniform akin to that of the Fae ahead. She pushed down her dismay: there was nothing for it, she would *have* to try and bluff it out.

"I uh, forgot my..." she gestured vaguely at her neck, "...you know."

The Fae gave her a curious smile that made her think he didn't believe her in the slightest, but he said: "With me, then, sweeting: I'll get you through safe."

"Thank you," said Dion, with real gratitude. She was somewhat taken aback when the Fae swept her beneath his cloak and wrapped his arm around her waist, thus drawing her forward and through the gate. Dion was left with her head out of the cloak, very close to the Fae's own, and when the guards' eyes lingered on her, smirking, she flushed hot and red. One of the wagoneers gave her a sympathetic look, but firmly grasped the arm of his young companion, who had started to rise from the seat beside him. Fortunately, they were soon beyond the leers of the guards, but just as Dion was beginning to expect the Fae to release her into the wide, main street of Bithywis, he irresistibly bore her down one small, winding road– and then another that twisted even more worrisomely.

"Thank you!" she said, with something of a gasp. "But this is far enough. I can manage from here."

"We can't have you out on the main streets with no marker," said the Fae chidingly. "This way, sweeting!"

Dion, who had begun to resist in good earnest, was borne around the next corner in hands that seemed to have assumed the consistency of steel. She was thrown against a brick wall with a teeth-shaking jar, and the Fae stood back to observe her with amused eyes. They were in a suffocatingly pokey dead end, and the only way out was filled entirely by the Fae.

"Now, sweeting," he said. "I've been nice to you. It's your turn to be nice to me."

"L-let me pass," said Dion, refusing to clutch at her aching shoulder, which had met the wall first. "You're p-presuming on your uniform, sir."

"So proud!" said the Fae, in wondering tones. "It's no good throwing back your shoulders, sweeting; I can see your pretty lips trembling. I'm much nicer than the Watch House, you know. They're rough and really quite rude there."

Her voice scratchy and choked, Dion said: "You'll r-regret it if you don't let me go." There was a buzzing in her ears that threatened to swallow her, and a crease in her chin was trying to make her cry. But behind it all there was the hot, full sensation of magic building, hidden and potent.

The Fae didn't seem to see it: perhaps he was used to Fae magic, or perhaps she was merely doing a very good job of hiding it. He said: "We'll start with a kiss first, I think. Don't kick me, sweeting, or I assure you that it will be much more...unpleasant...for you."

He moved forward as he spoke, with a swift, snake-like movement of his arm for her waist; and Dion, snake-like herself, struck. The Fae was thrown violently back into the next street as a bolt of raw magic punched into his chest, his purple eyes blank and wide. She saw recognition and deadly determination in those eyes as he tried to rise again, and called the stones to hold him. He sank into the street immediately, flailing in panic, and although Dion knew that a Fae wouldn't escape the clutches of stone very easily, she ran for her life, her breath ragged in her throat.

She managed to halt her mad, panting progression just before she burst into the main street again. Wriggling into a small, walled garden where the gap between gate and brick wall was just a little too big to prevent visitors, she tucked herself behind a tree and tried to think. There was something very wrong in Bithywis. Tokens of citizenship hadn't been seen in centuries, and Dion was very well aware that no laws had been passed to that effect, either. There had been a bill, quite a long time ago, requiring aliens and non-citizens to carry a mark of their status, but this was something quite different. All the humans she had seen were clearly Llassarian stock: they were tall, either pale or ruddy with their white skin, and hair inclined to curling. There was no reason for any of them to be displaying a non-resident marker.

Dion stayed where she was, cold and unsure, until the light of the evening began to fade. She would have liked to think that it was for purely strategical reasons—she would be harder to see after dark—but she was quite well aware that it was simply because she was afraid. When she did finally slither back under the garden gate, it was with a carefully constructed glamour in place, despite the cover of darkness. That glamour, as uncomfortable as it made her feel, was the glamour of a Fae. She hadn't seen any Fae wearing the markers, and while she wasn't yet willing to consider why that was, it seemed safer to glamour as if she was from Faery. People were less willing to accost Fae. Even lesser Fae had a formidable amount of magic and were dangerous targets, no matter how foolhardy the assailant. As Dion walked the main street of Bithywis, her eyes darting from side to side in fear that the Fae guard would still appear, it seemed that she was not the only one who considered the night streets safer for Fae. In her carefully casual stroll along the cobbled road, Dion saw many Fae, bright and dark, glittering and dangerous, laughing and enjoying the night. Of humans, she had not a single sight. Were the streets of Bithywis so dangerous that none but Fae dared to walk them? And if so, why had she not seen official paperwork– requests for succour and help from the Crown?

Dion knew her mother and father would have sent special troops to assist if they were needed.

The town hall was closed when Dion approached it; and, made wary by her encounter with the Fae guard, she couldn't bring herself to approach the Watch House for help, Royal Seal or no. That being the case, thought Dion a little desperately, the best thing to do was to find somewhere safe for the night, and get off the street. It was no doubt her fear speaking, but she seemed to hear footsteps behind her that slowed when she slowed, and stopped when she stopped. When Dion looked over her shoulder she couldn't see anyone following her, but the feeling of being watched didn't abate. She retraced her steps to the lower main street, where she'd first passed by alehouses and inns, and chose the smallest, most modestly lit inn. Its windows were low to the cobbled streets and Dion descended four stairs to gain entrance, which pleased her insofar as she was capable of pleasure at the time. Casual passers-by were unlikely to take any notice of her sitting at one of the taphouse tables when her head was somewhere in the region of their ankles. Dion didn't particularly feel like eating, but she knew from past experience that as little as she might feel like eating in unpleasant circumstances, it was always advisable to eat anyway. She had to duck her head to enter but once inside the ceiling was high enough not to feel as though it was crushing her.

Dion knew too much about being unnoticed to try and skulk in the shadows. Instead, she kept her light Fae glamour and sat at one of the window booths, wearing face #30– polite, distant unconcern. She ordered a small meal and when it arrived she ate it methodically, despite the leaden way it sat in her stomach. Her neck ached with stifling the urge to look around every few moments, and after her meal arrived, she used the window as a glass to see what was happening around her. Thanks to her Fae glamour, no one had given her more than a passing glance. Dion, automatically eating food that had no savour or taste, was free to be bewildered by her thoughts and impressions, and soon forgot to look in the glass at all.

What had happened in Bithywis? It was a completely different proposition from the town she had driven through and stopped in briefly to be presented with a ceremonial birthday present. Where were the beautifully decorated shop-fronts; the air of festivity; the bunting in royal colours? Where had the humans gone? So far Dion had seen only Fae. In fact, there was an air of alienness to the whole town, a creeping sort of feeling that crawled up her neck and scratched at her scalp. It wasn't just the Fae guard who had accosted her, it was in the very bricks and awnings and even in the sparkling cleanliness of the alehouse around her. Everything sparkled a bit too bright; everything was a bit too reflective. There was a cold, distant kind of handsome-ness even to the fire, which didn't manage to warm her as it should have.

A door opened and closed, bringing with it a swift draught of cool night air. Dion shivered in her window-booth, and felt something warm and sinewy slide around her shoulders. A shock of numbing confusion seized her, but when she opened her mouth in a shriek of protest it was immediately and forcibly silenced by the pressure of lips against her own. Dion found herself thrust against the window and unable to move; her arms pinned to her sides by two iron-like ones in green, her ankles pinched painfully against the corner by a leather boot, and her head trapped immovably between the booth corner and person who was kissing her. There was nothing she could do, in fact, except be kissed.

In the midst of her panic, Dion's first thought was, *What would Aerwn do?* Unfortunately, the single answer that question inspired was that Aerwn would kiss the stranger back, so Dion went with the second, which was to bite down as hard as she could bring herself to do on the stranger's lower lip. She tasted blood, terri-fied and elated at once, and the stranger released a gasp of slightly ale-scented breath. Then he purred a lascivious *"Ow!"* in Dion's frightened and astonished ear, and added: "Do that again and I'll tell everyone in the house about that clever glamour you're wearing. *Don't* scream."

"Get *off*!" panted Dion, her cheeks hot and red. There was a buzzing of magic in her fingers but she didn't dare let it loose while she was so surrounded by other patrons. "I won't scream, get off, get *off*!"

He pulled back without quite moving far enough away, and Dion found that she was being laughed at by a pair of very bright blue eyes in an almost stunningly handsome face. Her face went even redder, and she said chokingly: "Go *away*!"

"Oh, cherry, but then I wouldn't be able to enjoy your beautiful colour!" he said.

Dion self-consciously wiped blood from her mouth, aware that the stranger was still watching her with laughing eyes and a curling smile. He didn't seem to feel the need to wipe the blood from *his* lips, and Dion, averting her eyes, said again: "Please go away."

"Well, now," he said, "if you hadn't started to scream when I sat down beside you, I wouldn't have had to kiss you."

"I didn't want you to sit next to me!" gasped Dion, needled into looking up again.

"Don't be like that, cherry," he said. "I was curious to know why a human girl is wearing a Fae glamour, and it didn't seem likely that you'd want attention drawn to it. If you hadn't squeaked when I put my arm around you, I wouldn't have had to silence you. Fae don't notice an interlude, but they do dislike shrieking."

"We're not having an interlude!" said Dion, flushing even deeper red than before. She *hadn't* been imagining that someone was following her.

"Are we not?" he asked, licking the blood from his lips salaciously.

"Don't do that!"

He laughed softly and infectiously. "You're just too much fun to tease, cherry. What are you doing out and about without your owner? I'll not inform on you, mind."

Dion gaped at him, even more bereft of words than his kiss had made her. At last, she said in a hiss: "No one *owns* me! What has happened in Bithywis?"

The stranger stared down at her, frowning; then put his arm around her again and ducked his head.

"No!" said Dion, a furious heat of magic rising in the hand that shoved against his chest.

He hissed and pulled away, but said: "All right, cherry, I'm not going to kiss you again. Tilt your chin up and smile at me, then lean your head into my shoulder. And keep your voice down."

Dion, flexing her fingers and safe in the knowledge that she was prepared to attack if need be, did as she was told. She found herself shielded from the rest of the room by the stranger's shoulders.

"We're going to talk very, *very* quietly," he said. "You're as green as a new bean, think on! Where are you from? What's your name?"

"I'm D—" Dion caught herself up just in time, and finished lamely: "Di. I'm Di. I'm from beyond Llassar."

"Well, Di from beyond Llassar, I'm Padraig. It's a happy thing you fell in with me, or you might have fallen in with trouble."

Dion was rather certain that she'd fallen into enough trouble with Padraig but didn't quite like to say so. Instead, she said: "What's going on here? Has the town been overtaken?"

She already knew it hadn't been overtaken: the Fae guard had been easy and practised in his assault, as if he had done it many times before, and his uniform was that of Llassarian guards. Padraig himself spoke as if this...this *madness* was nothing new.

"Ah, it's a history lesson you're wanting, is it?" said Padraig, his eyes glittering in the reflected light from the windows. "Well, then; it started with the opening of the rifts. Would you be knowing of *those?*"

"Everyone knows about the rifts," she said, brushing the back of one hand against her cheeks. They still felt hot and stiff.

"I didn't like to assume," he said, with a slight gleam of white teeth. "Well now, it wasn't long before Fae found the rifts and began to come through. They claimed they were running from a great evil, a group of Elder Fae—powerful, ancient beings—known as the Guardians. Fae they are, just barely, but they have none of the same weaknesses as lesser Fae. Neither silver nor cold iron affect them a jot. Such a formidable people could be conveniently fashioned into an excuse to invade the world of men. There have always been Fae who slipped through and lived in the human world, but this was a different matter."

"They sent ambassadors," said Dion, dismissing the implication that heavily laced Padraig's flow of words.

"Aye, ambassadors were sent and accepted; treaties were signed and sealed. There was a steady flow of outcast Fae through and around us, and we were sent our portion as the Crown decreed. Houses were built, a portion of the town's water and stock-land was set aside, and the Fae were among us."

"Didn't the local population welcome them?" It wouldn't surprise Dion: there were some towns who had protested and written great, official letters to the Crown declaring their unwillingness to take in the outcasts. Fae had been given the cold shoulder and made to feel unwelcome– a great shame on the people of Llassar, whom she had expected to behave with greater generosity and freeness of acceptance.

"Oh, aye," said Padraig, the ghost of a smile hovering about his mouth. "We welcomed them. Had a parade, mark you! We tossed flowers and sang, and saw them look down our noses at the display."

"I'm sure they didn't mean to be arrogant," Dion said uncomfortably. This was the sort of talk that Aerwn used to come out with. Already off-balance with Padraig, she began to feel as though she'd got herself into dreadful company. "They're used to such beautiful, magical things in Faery: our art and accomplishments must seem so– so *earthy* to them."

Dion was almost certain that Padraig's lip curled for the briefest moment. She had the uncomfortable feeling that he was one of the dissenters her parents had always cautioned her of: someone not to be spoken to, someone who could not be argued with, someone who would always pull a well-meaning advisor down to his level. The fingers of her other hand began to warm with the cautious growth of magic.

"Aye, perhaps so," he said dryly. "And yet, one day we went about our lives in peace, a Llassarian town of mingled humans and Fae outcasts. The next we woke to find that we were slaves, our rights taken away and our king and queen either powerless or unwilling to stop it. We stood against it, but the law was changing and we found ourselves on the wrong side of it."

Dion had the sensation of being stuck in a dream. Of all the high-flown rhetoric to use! *Slaves* and *outlaws*?

"And worse, in Shinpo and Montalier," he added significantly. "Or have you forgotten the atrocities committed in our neighbouring countries, Di from beyond?"

"Those are the violent Fae," she protested. "The Unseelie, who love to make trouble, and the desperate! They don't speak for the rest of the Fae, and the rest of the Fae don't accord with them."

"Violence or not, it makes no odds," said Padraig. There was an impatience and an air of exasperation to his voice that stung Dion: she wasn't being unreasonable, neither was she lacking in intelligence. "You'll have it that the horrors these Fae perpetrate is the end in itself: something the deranged enjoy, and the desperate engage in unwillingly. It's not. It's a means to an end. What almost all Fae have in common is the desire to rule both the human and the Fae worlds according to their own will."

Dion tried to protest at the absurdity of it, but he ignored her. "Some of them accomplish that through law, and accord, and friendly means that mask their intent until it's too late. Some of them think it beneath them to treat with the humans and are assured of their right to take what they will, when they will. Thus we have towns and countries taken over by force."

"That's ridiculous!" Dion said, when she got her breath back. "How can you think such a thing?"

"Think it! I live it! Who are you, Di from beyond, to tell me that my experiences are ridiculous?"

Dion, flustered, said: "I didn't! I said–"

"We live under the thumb of the Fae in Bithywis," said Padraig. "As do they in the Shinpoan villages that were taken by force. There humans may not take to the streets without their owners or their token of self-ownership. They're forced to keep to curfew, and to line up in the streets for their daily ration of food. We do the same here. Should we be grateful that our over-throw came by way of deceitful smiles instead of honest violence?"

"I don't believe you," Dion said quietly, her face as white as her muslin sleeves. "Humans forced to wear a sign of their humanity? To apply for a ration of food? The king and queen would never allow it!"

Padraig said softly: "That's the way of it, is it? Follow me, then, cherry. You'll see soon enough."

"I'm n-not going anywhere with you!"

"Must I threaten you again, cherry?"

Dion withdrew into herself as far as she was able, hunching away from Padraig's surrounding warmth. "T-tell them if you must," she said, and made a stiff effort to raise her chin. "I'm not going anywhere with you."

Padraig looked down at her sharply, and said with unexpected gentleness: "Who hurt you, cherry? Tell me who he is and I'll make him pay for it."

"I already made him pay," said Dion, in a tight, proud voice. "And you did worse, anyway."

"*I* did? What, that chaste kiss?"

"It wasn't at *all* chaste!" Dion said. Her voice was shaking again, she knew. "And you had n-no business forcing it on me, even if it was!"

Was that a slight touch of red high in his cheeks? There was certainly a deep line between his brows. "I've badly bungled the thing," he said. "I was expecting you to be a wee bit different, think on. Sure, I thought you'd hit me! I'd not have kissed you like that if I'd known– ach, I shouldn't have done it at all. Forgive me, cherry. It was badly done."

"Oh," said Dion. She looked at him properly this time, and couldn't see a trace of guile to his eyes. She sat a little straighter and said at last: "All right. I forgive you."

A smile lit Padraig's face at once. "You're such a lovely, soft thing," he said. "Can I kiss you again?"

"N-no!" said Dion, thrown off balance once more.

"Now I really am curious," he said, his eyes still bright and interested. "What did you do to your attacker, cherry?"

"Threw him across the street," said Dion. "Imprisoned him in the cobbles."

She flushed as Padraig hissed appreciatively, his mouth pursed. "Aye, I *knew* I'd like you, Di from beyond! Come with me. I swear I'll not touch you again."

He rose as he spoke and Dion rose with him without really thinking about it. "Where are we going?"

"Somewhere we can have a sociable drink or two and a bit of a chat," said Padraig. "It's a bonny night and 'twould be a shame to spend it all in the one place."

He pulled Dion's hand through his arm as though they were a couple on an outing, and Dion, who hadn't quite dismissed the magic that was gathered at her fingertips, still let it simmer below the skin. As they left the inn together, he looked her up and down very frankly, making her blush again, and said: "You're a pleasant companion, to be sure!"

"Your accent isn't Llassarian," said Dion, by way of trying to keep her composure. She wished the night wasn't quite so well-lit with moonlight: it was harder to assume an Expression when she could feel the warmth of blood in her cheeks and know that it was visible.

"Well-spotted," said Padraig, not at all thrown. "You could say that I'm from beyond as well: my parents weren't Llassarian and I seem to have taken their trick of speaking. Well now, Di from beyond, in your walkings about earlier, did you happen to take note of the signs?"

"It *was* you following me!"

Padraig grinned, his eyes dancing. "Would I be doing such a thing? Did I not see a beautiful young thing who seemed to have lost her way, and out of the goodness of my heart attend her until she reached safe haven?"

"You– *why* did you follow me?"

"I told you, cherry. I was curious to know why such a beautiful young thing was out alone after dark– and wearing a Fae glamour, no less! I'm still anxious to know about that glamour, mind: I've not seen its equal. It could almost have fooled even me."

Dion frowned. How *had* Padraig seen through her glamour? There was barely a touch of magic to him: a tiny spark that was so small she couldn't even tell what kind of magic it was. He could be funnelling the miniscule flare into anything from charm to insight, but nothing more than that, and barely that. She was still wondering about it when she realised that they had paused before a notice in one of the shop windows. It was lettered in Fae cursive, beautiful and sprawling, and she had seen much the same thing in each window without taking notice of the fact.

She read it without meaning to—almost without comprehending it—and her eyes flitted on to the next few posted notices in shocked silence.

"There now," said Padraig. "Do you read the Fae script, cherry?"

"Yes," said Dion, through a closed throat. She was very familiar with the curved script and its once-foreign words. This particular sign read: *No human custom. Fae only.* Scratchily, she said: "Perhaps they were having difficulties with human customers."

Padraig's smile was lazy. "Aye, and I suppose every second business has the same problem? Walk with me, cherry. Look to the storefronts."

"I see them," she said. Worse, she had seen the other flyers in the shop window– the ones that offered *sale of services: two young humans 1xm, 1xf, useful for manual labour and some skilled applications* or simply *middle-aged human available: high millinery skills, fully broken in.* She could feel the shivering start the way it always did: the sickness, the numbness, the nightmare heaviness of it all.

"You're trembling, cherry," said Padraig, frowning. "Are you cold?"

"No," said Dion, through numb lips. "Don't worry about it. It won't stop anyway. Where are we going?"

She was aware of his eyes on her for quite some time before he said: "Not far now. No, no, *this* way: we want something Seelie and grand."

So saying, he steered Dion away from a modest, quiet establishment that she had instinctively moved toward, and swept her onward until they were on the cusp of a great, golden facade. Dion, her eyes dazzled, took in the light of a conjured sun that slowly rose and sank across the front wall, casting an almost daylight aspect on the street below. Like all the most beautiful of Seelie things, the warmth of it didn't quite reach her skin, let alone the cold, inner part of her that fed her shivering fits.

Padraig slid his arm around her waist, his short cloak draping over her shoulders as well, and when Dion twitched herself away he murmured: "Best they not see you trembling, cherry."

Still, he didn't try to put his arm around her again until she came closer, and she let the last of her built-up magic sink back down.

They approached the tap counter, much to Dion's foreboding. There were many other patrons also lounging at their ease by the counter; some Unseelie, but more Seelie. Padraig threw himself into a seat, nodding casually at the golden Fae closest to them, and pulled Dion in close against him, her shivering covered by his cloak and growing a little less in his warmth. He ordered drinks for both of them and said, "Well met," to the Seelie Fae, who returned the greeting languorously.

"Beautiful night, to be sure."

"Inasmuch as night can be said to be beautiful," shrugged the Seelie, with a faint lift of his lip. "The human world has many attractions, but this passion for dreary darkness is not one of them."

"Darkness has its charms," said Padraig.

The Seelie Fae laughed. "For those with the taste for it. I am for the sunshine."

"Aye, I thought the days were a smidgen longer than they had been," said Padraig incomprehensibly. "What news of Illisr? I had heard they were tending to the dark, but it's been some time since I heard tell of them."

"Is it so?" the golden Fae's brows rose. "You've missed a great deal. Illisr is over-run this last year—plunged into darkness—and Shinpo is half-spent as well, cut at the ankles and floundering. It's said the royal family was taken in the night a day ago: Shinpoans are fighting a separated battle across the country, unable to rally enough to make a convincing effort."

"That's news indeed," said Padraig, lifting his tankard. He seemed to be drinking, but Dion, used to giving herself a few moments to prepare her reactions, was aware that he was surprised and dismayed at the news. What did Padraig care for Illisr and Shinpo? The news had affected him in a personal way, and not merely as an unfortunate piece of news.

"Such a pity!" sighed the golden Fae. "Illisr has such a wealth of art and commodity: to see it attacked in such a way is dreadful. And Shinpo! Such spices! Such delicate fabrics!"

Dion wasn't unaware of the unrest the surrounded the Fae incursion of the human world. Like her parents she had considered the peril the Fae were fleeing as passport enough to the help and succour of Llassar; but not every country surrounding them had thought so. Montalier and Shinpo had both declined to take Fae into their cities, and Illisr had taken them only conditionally. Some of the more powerful Fae, taking exception to the exclusion, had begun to wage violent and insidious warfare against them, fighting for their less powerful Seelie and Unseelie brethren. Her father had refused to allow her to visit those countries, his righteous anger aroused against their selfish outlook and unwillingness to help, but Dion received enough information of the three countries during her tutored schooling to feel that she had a good idea of what was happening around the world. It was unfortunate, of course, that Montalier, Shinpo, and Illisr were experiencing such violence, but their policy had brought a vast measure of it upon themselves. The Fae were desperate, and had acted desperately.

This Seelie Fae was refreshingly moderate. Dion felt an almost crushing relief: she had seen and heard such things today that had made her despair of Bithywis and almost, but not quite, of Llassar itself.

"Barbarians!" said the Seelie Fae, his golden voice disgusted. "Using brute force and magic to overcome prejudice! There are more civilised ways of bringing the world into alignment. Witness what has been done so successfully in Llassar: a Fae-led country where Fae and humans live side by side, with everyone in their place and the proper distinguishing of rank."

Dion felt a sinking in her heart; a quivering deep in her soul.

"Aye," said Padraig, his voice soft and dangerous. "And what distinguishing would that be, my pretty Fae?"

The Seelie Fae looked faintly surprised. "The Fae are superior to humans in every conceivable way—your own blood and lineage must tell you so!—in every aspect of mind, magic, judgement and physical prowess. Their laws are inferior, their abilities more so: it was a happiness to them when we took the reins of government in Llassar."

"You'd best tell them that," said Padraig, with a sharp kind of bitterness. "To be sure, they seem to have forgotten!"

"I see it's no use talking to you," the Seelie Fae said, his thin nostrils flared. "Your kind ought to be outlawed as well."

"No doubt your kind will see to that quickly enough," Padraig said, his teeth showing in a humourless grin. "We'd best go, cherry. I think we've outworn our welcome."

Dion stumbled through the door with him; and she thought, amidst all the bravado and affected unconcern, that Padraig wasn't quite steady himself. When they were away from the cold light of the Seelie establishment's conjured sun, he said softly: "I'm sorry, cherry. But you had to know, think on."

"Yes," said Dion. Some time between sitting down and leaving the inn she had begun to shake worse than ever, and she could feel the familiar, deathly weariness creeping up her limbs. "I need– I have to rest now."

"This way, then," said Padraig. He must have seen her chin rise and her shoulders straighten, because he didn't try to put his arm around her again. "I've somewhere safe to stash you."

Dion knew the rest of the night in a blurred nightmare. Padraig took her somewhere that smelled of fire and iron and put her to sleep on a small, truckle-bed in one corner of a darkened room. He would have stayed and talked—she even thought he was about to sit beside her and pull her close—but Dion, shivering beneath the blanket and as sick with anxiety and wrong as she had ever been, said: "I'll be better tomorrow."

He might have said something else to her, but Dion had lost consciousness by then. She slept deeply and entirely uselessly, and awoke the next day with heavy eyes and a heavier heart. Padraig was already awake, adding the scents of tea and toast to those of fire and iron. He glanced over at her when she sat up, and she was thankful to note that though he obviously saw the heaviness of her eyes, the shaking had stopped.

"You'd best eat," he said. "I've a feeling you need the energy. You're a mite delicate, I think."

"No, just stupid," said Dion, very much aware of the wedge of desolation sitting squarely in her stomach. "I've been like it since I was a child. I don't...*react*...well. It's not very comfortable."

"I wouldn't have thought so," said Padraig, flipping a piece of bread on the toasting fork. "Is there nothing that can give you relief?"

"Yes," said Dion, without thinking about it; and then: "No," because she wasn't inclined to mention Barric. "Sometimes I can pretend it isn't there for long enough to hide it, but it makes me so *tired*."

"That must be inconvenient for a princess," said Padraig.

Dion, with a buzz of shock, looked up and met his eyes. She mechanically took the plate and teacup that he proffered and said: "When– *how* did you know?"

"Ah, I've known from the beginning," he said. He sat down beside her, very much at his ease, a teacup clasped loosely between his fingers. "A friend of mine said you'd be here yesterday and asked me to look out for you. She seemed to think you needed to see a few things."

"Aerwn!" said Dion. She drew in a deep breath, slowly and shakily. "Oh, *Aerwn*! What did they do to her? And I thought– they said– oh! Poor Aerwn!"

"Ah, she's a tough nut enough," said Padraig easily. "Takes a lot to rattle that one."

"You didn't see her after she came back from Doctor Whishte," said Dion unhappily. "I thought she was lying! She lied so much!"

"Aye," said Padraig. "I told her it would backfire on her, but she was ever a determined little beast."

Dion, finishing a tasteless morsel of toast, said: "I have to get back as quickly as possible."

"You've much to see: a week or two won't make a difference," he said. "Except to your people, mind. They need to see that you're willing to help."

"I see," said Dion. There was evidently a purpose and plan in place that had been so for some time. She owed it to Aerwn—not to mention the human Llassarians—to see the venture out. At length, she said: "Thank you."

"What for?"

"Your honesty. I didn't believe you and you told me the truth anyway. Thank you."

Padraig's face lit with a smile. "Oh aye, I'll always tell you the truth, your highness."

"You might as well stick with Di," said Dion, flushing a little. "You've saved my life, after all.

"Well now," said Padraig. "Isn't this a pleasant thing! Will you be going back to the coach?"

"No, I don't think so," Dion said. "Will the Fae be awake again?"

"Not likely," said Padraig. He was grinning. "I used vaporised iron: it takes a good deal of heat, but it knocks them out until their lungs can be pumped."

Dion frowned down into her cooling tea. "Vaporised iron is poisonous to humans, isn't it?"

"Aren't you the clever one! Indeed it is: I was told you would have a spell on your person to protect against such things."

"What if I hadn't been wearing my travel wrap?" asked Dion, in fascination. "You would have been responsible for murdering the heir to Llassar's throne!"

"Killing, at the very worst!" protested Padraig. "And involuntary killing, too! I'd scarcely see a decade of prison food."

"It was in the lanterns, wasn't it? Iron in the casings and something to make the Fae-lights overheat–"

"Indeed it was. Where did you learn about vapourised metals in a Fae-tutored schoolroom?"

"That wasn't in the schoolroom," said Dion, going pink at Padraig's distinctly admiring tones. "I used to visit the library a lot. I always had questions that the tutor didn't answer and I didn't like to cause a fuss."

"What did they do when they found out?"

Dion blinked a little. It hadn't occurred to her until now that anyone had *found out*, but now that she came to think of it, a little while after her fourteenth birthday there had been a fire in the royal library. At the time she had believed the story that someone had merely been too careless with a lantern.

"There was a fire," she said, hunching her shoulders. "They said someone knocked over one of the lanterns. Only– only we didn't have lanterns in the library. It was all Fae lighting by then. I wasn't allowed in the library for months after that, and when I did get back in, half the books were missing." *The Song of the Broken Sword* was one of those that was missing. Dion had never been so foolhardy as to climb the shelves again, but she knew it was gone because the Forbidden Books section was the worst damaged of the lot, and there was a charred, gaping hole where once *The Song of the Broken Sword* had been shelved.

"Aye, that has the scent of the Fae all over it," said Padraig. "They like to do things indirectly when they can: they enjoy playing with their humans."

Dion said quietly: "I suppose we should feel ourselves fortunate that the Fae who came to Llassar took over by stealth rather than by violence. The end result has been the same, but at least here there hasn't been such great loss of life."

"Stealth? No. By legislation and trickery and manipulation of feeling. Our deaths may not have been so violent, but they have been as numerous. Not all of us welcomed the Fae taking over our towns, and there was some struggle."

"What happened?"

Padraig shifted his teacup between his hands. "We were slaughtered quickly, quietly, and entirely legally– with the full support of the Crown. Once the Fae were in such numbers that their votes counted for more than the rest of us, and once there were enough in the court to hold sway with the king and queen, our laws changed more quickly than we could keep up with. Some of us found ourselves on the wrong side of the law without meaning it; others of us thought it worth-while to become rebels and fight to save our families from slavery to the Fae."

"Were there no petitions made to the king and queen?" Dion had never seen any such. If there had been such, they could never have reached the king and queen– they would have been quick to avenge the wrongs of their people, even if those wrongs were perpetrated by the Fae.

"Oh, aye– once and again we sent messengers. First they were stopped on the roads, and when we sought to ally ourselves with the towns around us and send our distress together, it was outlawed."

"On what grounds?" cried Dion, nearly beside herself. Her parents *couldn't* be aware of this! And yet, how could they have been unaware? "To outlaw a citizen's right to petition with the Crown? How could such a thing happen?"

"Citizens still have the right to petition the Crown," Padraig said, with grim amusement. "Slaves, now; slaves have no such rights."

"Slavery was never a part of Llassar," Dion said, her throat tight. "Those signs I saw in the shop windows– has every human in Bithywis been enslaved?"

"Not so much enslaved as reassigned. The Fae are of the mind that humans are a bare step up from the animals, and that they need masters to keep them safe and in order."

"That Fae," said Dion, and she heard the tremble of anger in her voice that was almost a sob. She had never thought she could hate, but the tar of it in her throat almost choked her. "What did he mean about your lineage?"

Padraig shrugged. "Seelie Fae like to prick and cut where they can. He was trying to remind me of my place in this society of his."

"Why don't you have a token?"

"Ah, I'm a different thing altogether," said Padraig. "I don't fit into their little boxes so they leave me alone. Are you finished? There's something downstairs you'll be wanting to see."

The smell of soot and melted iron grew stronger as Padraig led Dion downstairs, but it wasn't until they left the house, stepping briefly through a narrow alley and straight into another door, that she realised why. They were in a forge. Dion, who had grown to recognise such places almost as sacrilegious, found that her first reaction was still shock, even though she knew better. She would have asked why they were in a forge, but she could already feel the magic emanating from the hammer and anvil that were close by the fire. They were potent, metallic sources of dusky magic, bound with a scarlet something that Dion thought might be a destiny cord. Whatever they were, the hammer and anvil were *important.*

Dion said: "*How?* How did you infuse *iron* with magic?"

"With some difficulty," admitted Padraig. "But it's not exactly iron, in a manner of speaking. It's more what you'd call an alloy. They call it steel: a bit of carbon in it, and the magic holds just fine."

"But that's *Fae* magic!"

"Aye, so it is," Padraig said, with a curious smile. "It's what you might call an alloy, too."

"I've never seen anything like it," Dion said in fascination. "It's so intricate and complicated!"

"Aye, but I'm a complicated fellow," said Padraig complacently. When Dion didn't answer, caught up in studying one of the most intricate webbings of magic that she had ever seen, he added: "See now, you're meant to giggle and flirt with me when I say a thing like that."

Dion was surprised into glancing at him. He winked at her, which made her look away again in confusion. She said hastily: "You're Coinnach's son, aren't you?"

"Ah, so there was a bit of teaching done! I am. We're partners in this world-saving venture."

"It will be a pity for these to be used up," said Dion, running her fingers over the anvil.

"Aye," said Padraig; and there was that odd smile again. "And 'twill be a pity for–"

"For me to die?" said Dion, when he stopped short. "There's always Aerwn. Llassar won't be left wanting."

"You know you're to die?" said Padraig, visibly startled. "Who would be telling you such a thing?"

"I've known since I was seven," Dion said. He was still looking at her fixedly, and she knew why. She said, with a flush: "It's all right. I'm not going to collapse again."

"Now there's a curious thing," he said, gazing at her with such an affectionate sadness that it was hard to meet his eyes. "Sure, Aerwn did tell me you were the better twin. Last night you were all but incapacitated when you saw the evil that had come on your people. Today you tell me you are to die without the slightest quiver in your voice."

"I've had a long time to get used to it," said Dion quietly. "And it's different. I know what I have to do. But with the Fae–" she trailed off in despair. "This, all of this: it's our fault, the whole royal family of Llassar. *We* did this. My blindness– my parents'– well, I don't know. But we allowed it. We even welcomed it. I can't see how that can ever be repaired."

"Well now, that's what we'll be doing, isn't it? You and I, saving the world. We'll have a bonny time of it, Di from beyond."

THEY CREPT QUIETLY from town to town over the next two weeks, working their way carefully toward Harlech. Padraig seemed to be known in every town, and in every town there were signs of quiet, careful organisation that chilled Dion to the bone. It was almost as terrible to consider as the icy grip of the Fae that held the country in thrall. It promised that, barring quick, decisive change, Things Would Be Done. Fae and Llassarians would be at war; and worse, the royal family would be on the wrong side.

During the day they travelled and talked. By night they stayed in a series of homes that welcomed them under cover of darkness and sent them away before the dawn broke. It made Dion wonder exactly how well known Padraig was around Llassar, and exactly what would happen were they to draw the attention of any of the increasing numbers of Fae guards she saw as they got closer to Harlech. Her uneasiness was only doubled by the presence of two very visible reminders of their quest: Padraig's anvil, made small by some extension of its enchantment, hung from his neck by a chain while his hammer swung from his belt. As obvious as they were to Dion, she was constantly fearful of the Fae discovering them.

With every Fae guard, every insult, every instance of brutality and wrong to Llassarian humans that she saw, Dion grew sicker and angrier. By the time they reached Harlech in the cool of late afternoon two weeks later, she was by no means prepared to sneak in by darkness and return to the castle by stealth.

"Aye, well, who can blame you?" said Padraig, with half a smile. "Here is where my journey ends, then."

"But–" *But I wanted to present you to my parents.* That was no good. "My parents will want–"

"Your parents will want to hang me from the closest gibbet," said Padraig. "And the Fae will want to– well, they're an unpleasant lot. Here is where we kiss and part, cherry."

Much to Dion's embarrassment, he did kiss her. This time he gave her ample time to pull away if she wished, and to her further embarrassment, Dion didn't do so. In an effort to hide her confusion, she said: "Will you go back to Bithywis?"

"I think not," said Padraig, with an amused smile at her red cheeks. "I'll be around for a while. If you need me, tell Aerwn to get a message to me."

He was gone in an instant, melting into the streets at the very moment the gate guards saw Dion. They snapped to attention, their Fae eyes wide and worried, and Dion set her shoulders. It was time to go to battle.

DION ENTERED the Court of Affairs at a good time: the king and queen were presiding over the citizens' complaints—of which, she was very well aware, there were seldom any—and it was the easiest thing in the world to join the line of three other citizens. The citizens were all Fae, she noticed with a bitter smile. They all hesitated, but as the entire court came to attention Fae reluctantly moved aside, and Dion swept before her parents in all her travel-weariness and dirt. She was a little sorry not to see Aerwn attending, but then, Aerwn rarely did attend; something that no longer surprised Dion.

"Daughter!" said the queen gladly. "We are glad to see you home safely! We received news that you had lengthened your tour."

"Yes," said Dion, and heard the tremble in her voice. "Yes. I did."

"I see you have news," said the king in indulgent but slightly reproving tones. "We will be glad to hear it, but this is not the place."

"No," Dion said. Her voice was louder, and though it was rough around the edges it didn't tremble this time. She saw the Fae around the court moving in a watchful, worried flow of movement, a breeze of unease sweeping through them. "No, this is exactly the place. As a citizen of Llassar, I bring a complaint to the Crown, and as heir to the Crown, I bring with me the complaint of my people."

Tutor Halfhelm, her instructor in foreign affairs, hurried up to her, exclaiming: "You are fatigued, your highness! Surely a moment can be taken to sit down and refresh yourself. You are disordered and confused!"

"Stay away from me!" said Dion, in such a savage tone that Halfhelm stopped at once. "I will not rest while my people are unrepresented."

"My dear!" said the queen, her face dismayed. "You're weeping! You must sit down! We can meet again after you've rested: we'll speak in private."

Dion, aware of the furious tears rolling down her cheeks but unable to do anything about them, said: "We'll speak in public, and now. My carriage broke down outside Bithywis two weeks ago. My Fae attendants were rendered unconscious and I was left to walk back to Bithywis alone. I spent a night and a day there unknown, and saw humans enslaved while their Fae masters live on the best of the land."

The king stood, white and wrathful. "My daughter attacked and nothing of it discovered?"

The captain of the guard, a smooth, beautiful Fae in glossy leather armour, stepped forward. "Your Majesty, there was the question of a ransom demanded," she said, bowing. The grace of the action couldn't hide its insolence in Dion's eyes. "The Princess's abduction was discovered a bare week and a half ago, and it was thought best to return her to your majesties without worrying the queen or further disordering Princess Aerwn."

"I wasn't kidnapped," said Dion. Beside the captain's assured, melodious tones, her voice sounded small and weak. "There was an attack, but I escaped. It isn't important."

"We received a ransom demand," said the captain; politely, smilingly insistent. She approached Dion with a measured tread, so powerfully smiling and polite that Dion felt almost physically battered. "An anti-Fae group, your Majesties. They are well known for aggression toward Fae citizens. Undoubtedly the princess has been frightened to within an inch of her life and is repressing these unpleasant memories with something easier to understand."

"Let the girl speak!" said a sharp, whip-crack of a voice. It belonged to Duc Owain ap Rees, and Dion found herself spurred into life again. "Are the Fae so afraid of one young girl?"

"You forget yourself, ap Rees," said the king dangerously; but he sat down. "Speak, daughter. What is this foolishness?"

"Look at her!" exploded Tutor Halfhelm. "She's beside herself with fatigue! She needs to rest!"

"This comes of being held captive for two weeks," said Tutor Iceflame coldly. "On a weak mind, pressure and repetition produce every kind of evil. She has been brainwashed, your Majesty. I must take some of the blame for also having neglected to tell you the true state of affairs. Please believe me that I was with the captain, working constantly to find and free the princess."

"I am not beside myself and I am not brainwashed," said Dion, her voice cracking. "I am angry. My people have been reduced to chattel and enslaved to the very Fae we welcomed with open arms! I have *seen it with my own eyes*. Humans tagged like cattle and forced to queue in the streets for their daily food. Fae who feel themselves free to assault and offend where it pleases them."

There was a growl of anger around the room, but Dion,

looking for a moment into Duc Owain ap Rees' stern, approving eyes, took fresh courage. "Human Llassarians have appealed to the courts and directly to the Crown but have been denied or prevented."

"Daughter, you are beside yourself," said the king. There was a sternness in his face, too; and Dion felt the first awful chill of knowledge. She swayed where she stood, and heard him say through a buzzing in her ears: "The human Llassarians have been weak and resentful. They have provoked and attacked until it was necessary to curb them. Their unsteadiness would have led to anarchy and death throughout Llassar. Do not think of them as under enslavement but under a benevolent guide for their own good. It is only through the wisdom of the Fae that Llassar will become great. Do not let me hear you speak in this manner again. Daughter though you may be, if you align yourself with the enemies of the Crown, you will suffer punishment with them."

A roar of approbation rose around the room and Dion sank to her knees, shivering, the world narrowing around her in a smothering darkness. She tried and failed to stand until an arm caught her around the waist, lifting her to her feet once again. The Duc ap Rees was beside her, his sinewy old arms bearing her up and lending strength.

"No," she said quietly. "Duc–"

"It's my honour to serve, your Majesty," he said. A few of the nearer Fae, hearing the title of address, hissed, but he ignored them with a stony face. In her ear, he said: "Finish your piece and shoulder the consequences. You are not alone."

Dion, raising her spinning head, said: "If the king and queen refuse to do what must be done to free our people, I will do it myself. The Fae will not have our land as they have the land of our neighbours."

There was a murmur among the Fae, soft at first, then louder. "Treason," it said; and then shouted: "Treason!"

The king rose again, this time with great heaviness. "Dion ferch Alawn, do you challenge the Crown?"

"No," said Dion. "I remind it of its duty to its people. I warn it that unless the Fae are removed and the Llassarian people free again, it will suffer dearly."

"The Fae are under our protection, daughter," said the king. "Do not speak against them."

"Treason!" came the many-voiced howl again. Dion saw the beautiful faces around her in their cold, satisfied fury. She had fallen, and they had won. "Treason to the Crown!"

"Dion ferch Alawn, you are charged with treason to the Crown," said her father. Dion looked to her mother and saw on her face a resolute kind of sorrow—an almost peaceful resignation—and gave herself up for lost. "In the presence of this court you have spoken threats to the Crown and treason against the Fae. You will be imprisoned overnight and executed tomorrow at noon."

DION WAS SHUT into the small, bricked holding room behind the Court of Affairs for an interminable time before she was hauled away to be locked up for the night. The carpeted halls didn't feel quite real beneath her feet as she was hurried along, nor did the lit fireplace in her newly acquired prison take away from the chill in the air.

She still seemed to hear the hisses and shouts of the Fae (or was that just the buzzing in her ears?); still seemed to feel the bruises around her elbows from the Fae guards who had torn her away from Duc Owain ap Rees as he roared and fought like a madman. She hadn't seen what happened to him. Dion crouched by the fire, her shaking fingers digging into the material of her overskirt and making holes in the material as her thoughts reeled over and over. She tried to tell herself that Owain was still alive, still safe, but the uncertainty of it ate away at her in imagination and sickness until she stumbled into the bathroom and lost the contents of her stomach in the bare bathroom.

When she returned to the main room, shivering and light-headed but able to make herself think again, Dion found it as rich and bare as the bathroom. It was one of the guest rooms, hurriedly stripped of anything useful for escape. The windows were bound with iron on the outside, as were all the windows this low in the castle, but the inner-facing glass had been bound with magic. In fact, the walls had all been threaded with binding magic, too; the strongest and most insidious of magic. Dion, gazing at it, recognised the work of her Instructor of Magic, and knew that she would lack the strength to break it until she was better rested.

If she looked through the keyhole of the locked door she knew she would only see the uniformed backs of the two Fae guards who had borne her grimly along with cruel fingers even though she didn't resist. It was no use trying to escape that way, either. Instead, Dion walked the floorb until the early hours of the morning, unable to sleep. She trembled bodily, weary and frightened. She was used to feeling uncertain and afraid, but there had always been the certainty of her mother and father, and of her position as Princess and Heir. Dion had always been certain that, destined to die as she was, she would yet be Queen first.

Instead, she was to die the death of a traitor. Worse, she could no longer cling to the hope that her parents were ensorcelled: she could see them before her eyes even now, not a scrap of magic in or around them. Fervour and sincerity in their eyes as they betrayed their own people and delighted in the alien Fae. Absolute righteousness in every line of their faces as they condemned her to prison, and after that to death.

Dion clasped her arms around herself and rocked in a desperation of regret. Her destiny to save the human world from the Fae had been nullified: her training, her magic, Barric's work– all in vain. Dion would have been certain just yesterday morning that nothing could happen to her; or at least, not until the fullness of time when, as Queen, she would give her life to seal up the land. And Aerwn? What of Aerwn? Who would look after her– who would *believe* her? Dion had seen the joyous satisfaction in the eyes of the court at her downfall, and she wondered how long it would be before her parents declared a Faery heir.

A time of darkness came over Dion, and when she recognised light and feeling again, she was crumpled on the rug before a dying fire. Her whole body was shaking in huge waves that sapped the strength from her limbs and added weight to the dreadful weariness that had overcome her. Into the silence of the room, her heart beat loud in a parody of heavy footfalls, beating a certain path of death and destruction for her people.

It was some time before Dion recognised that there really were approaching footsteps outside the door of her prison. There was a swift, precise scuffle on the other side of the door: the shifting of feet, two short, surprised grunts, and two soft thuds. Dion raised heavy eyes to the door but couldn't seem to gather together her leaden limbs. She would have liked at least to stiffen her spine, but everything was too fuzzy and soft, and Dion simply watched the door open without being able to do more than wonder dully if she was about to be taken to judgement. But it wasn't her Fae guards who appeared through the door: it was Barric, amazingly real and stunningly present.

"Barric," she said, catching her breath. "You're here. And *here*. Is it time to die?"

"It's time to go," said Barric. He picked her up gently, one arm supporting her knees and the other cradling her shoulders.

Dion's head lolled into his shoulder, her teeth chattering as convulsively as the rest of her. She said, with an effort: "Owain? The Duc? Have to get him *safe*–"

"The Duc is safe and well," said Barric. "A few bruises, nothing more. You and he still have a friend or two in the Court."

He kicked the door aside, stepping over the two fallen Fae guards, and Dion saw them briefly over his shoulder, pale and unconscious– or were they dead? She couldn't bring herself to feel anything for them, but she found that she was crying anyway. Barric hefted her slightly and Dion lost sight of the Fae, her sight curtailed to the single reality of his collar.

They passed through light and dark, sometimes walking, sometimes running. Soon Dion felt herself being carried below stairs and perhaps below ground, the air cool and dark around her. So Aerwn had been right: there *were* tunnels below the castle. Dion was aware of the world around her as in a dream, and in that dream, she heard Padraig's voice saying sharply: "Is she injured? Cherry, are you well?"

"Back, whelp," growled Barric.

Dion protested: "No! Padraig? Padraig, you're safe!"

"Of course, cherry!" he said, and Dion caught a glimpse of his laughing eyes over Barric's shoulder. "And I brought someone with me. Aren't I a darling?"

Aerwn was beside him, bouncing as she walked and kicking stones ahead of her without regard to noise. "Di, I heard all about it! Oh, what I wouldn't have given to see you shouting at them all!"

"I didn't shout," said Dion, rousing herself to gaze wonderingly at the rough-hewn stone ceiling that curved away over their heads.

"No, no, of course not. You talked to them in that furious little gruff voice that terrifies the life out of me, all the while with tears of rage pouring down your face."

Dion, lacking the energy or the need to protest what was, after all, largely true, simply said: "I'm glad you're safe."

"Oh, and he didn't bring me," Aerwn said, outpacing Barric with her energetic walk until Dion had to turn her head to see her sister. Padraig followed, still smiling at Dion, and Aerwn jerked her thumb at him. "*I* brought *him*."

Barric's eyes flickered toward her. "Get it?"

Aerwn's eyes sparkled back at him. "Got it!"

"What have you got?" asked Dion.

"The first shard, of course!" said her sister. "Don't tell me he didn't tell you about the shards! This one's been in the castle gardens for years with a little something to discourage Fae from getting too close."

"He told me," said Dion, blinking deep and long. There was a sharp, twisting feeling in her stomach that she didn't recognise. To Barric's collar, she said: "Were you teaching *Aerwn*, too?"

Barric glanced down at her, his scar pulling. "No. Only you."

"I had my own imaginary friend," said Aerwn. She threw an arm around Padraig's shoulders in a friendly fashion. "Padraig kept me company and showed me around. We had a few close scrapes, didn't we?"

Dion wasn't sure if that was any better than Aerwn being taught by Barric. When had she become so jealous of Aerwn?

"Just a few," said Padraig, with a rueful grin; but Dion thought she caught an apologetic look from him. She felt the shivers coming on again and tucked her head exhaustedly back into Barric's shoulder, trying to ignore Aerwn's entirely bright, entirely healthy presence.

Barric said: "You're underfoot. Go check the way."

"Which one of us?" demanded Aerwn, by no means pleased to be summarily sent off.

"Both," grunted Barric. Padraig didn't look any more pleased than Aerwn, but he followed her anyway, and they soon disappeared into the gloomy passage. Barric said softly: "Sleep if you can. You'll need your energy."

Dion said wearily: "I'm sorry. I hoped when the time came– I hoped I wouldn't be so weak."

Barric shrugged his huge shoulders. "Your strength lies within."

"No, it doesn't," said Dion, and found that there were tears slipping down her face again. "If you'd been able to talk to me about it earlier– if Aerwn had been able to confide in me– if I hadn't been so *blind*–"

She saw his scar jump, but not with a smile. "You trusted; and your honesty makes you see honesty in others. Loyalty and sense of honour are not to be ashamed of."

"Both of them were misplaced," said Dion quietly, and with bitterness. "Llassar will be well off with Aerwn as queen."

"Aerwn will be a good queen," said Barric. "Perhaps. In time. But Llassar can't be saved without you."

Dion said: "And Padraig's hammer and anvil," and let her head fall against his shoulder. A stubborn, clinging thought was nudging at her, and she gave voice to it. "I want– I want to see the Duc."

"Peace," said Barric's voice. "Ap Rees is out of Harlech this morning. He has an army to gather in readiness for their leader."

"This," she said. "All of this. It was poised on the edge of the precipice, just waiting for the last stone to fall. We're at war?"

"Yes," said Barric.

"Then it is...time to die," said Dion, and fell asleep.

3

THE BITTERNESS OF WINTER

*T*here was sunshine in Dion's eyes when she woke the next morning. Perhaps it was the sunshine that woke her. When she opened her eyes the first thing she saw was Padraig's face smiling down at her, and it seemed that the sunshine grew warmer. She couldn't help the smile that involuntarily curved her lips, and though the memory of the previous day rose immediately after, it wasn't quite enough to take away the lingering warmth when Padraig pulled her to her feet.

"Oh, for pity's sake!" said Aerwn's voice. She had been fixedly watching Barric make breakfast over a small fire, but now she made a face at Dion and Padraig. *"Don't* flirt with my sister, Padraig! It's disgusting!"

"Mind your own business, Aerwn," said Padraig, grinning in delight at the bright crimson that flooded Dion's cheeks. He murmured: "I missed you, cherry. You're looking bonny this morning."

Aerwn went back to staring at the breakfast, but she muttered: "Eugh! It's like watching my brother and sister flirt."

"You don't have a brother," said Dion, reluctantly pulling her hand out of Padraig's.

"Close enough," Aerwn grunted. "Feeling better, Di? You'd better eat something."

"I'm fine," Dion said, accepting the bowl that Barric silently passed to her. "Where are we?"

"Comfortably outside Harlech," said Padraig, as Dion walked a circle around the camp, automatically eating her porridge. "And nicely hidden, too, if it comes to that. Ywain was a fierce clever man."

"Yes," said Dion thoughtfully. Her eyes told her that they were in a circular ruin that was part of Old Harlech, perilously open and bare to prying eyes from Harlech's guard towers to the east and west. And yet, she could never quite *see* any of the guard towers; and if it came to that, although she could see Harlech's wall, she never managed to catch a sight of any part of the Guard Walk along the top of it. She looked closer at the skeletal brick remains around her and saw the faintest glimmer of the foundational magic that had gone into creating the effect. The ruins themselves weren't formed from magic; any Fae looking out over the wall from Harlech would have noticed that at first glance. No, Ywain—if it was he who had done it—had used magic to move actual bricks and hold them in place: in carefully constructed place, so that from the walls of Harlech it would have looked as though it were not capable of hiding a mouse. Every seemingly teetering spire of remnant brickwork was carefully positioned and painstakingly scaled to conceal the well-provisioned camp that it was.

"We came through tunnels," she said, frowning. She couldn't see anything like a tunnel entrance around them, but with the hidden perspectives and clever masonry, Dion wasn't prepared to swear that there *wasn't* one. "Or was that just a dream?"

"That was real," said Aerwn. She was bouncing on her toes in eagerness for her breakfast, but Barric's eyes were on Dion. Dion wasn't sure if he was deliberately baiting Aerwn or was merely waiting to see what Dion thought of the pretend ruins, but when she met his eyes he smiled faintly and passed a bowl to Padraig.

Dion said: "Where do we start, Barric? How do we begin to fight back?"

"Where's mine?" demanded Aerwn, seizing a bowl at the same time that Padraig said reproachfully: "Not over breakfast, cherry!"

"Dion likes to fix things as soon as she finds them broken," Aerwn said through a mouthful of porridge.

"Oh, that's beautiful," said Padraig, steering Dion to a seat beside his own chosen one.

"You said last night that Owain is gathering an army," Dion said to Barric. She could feel the trembling deep inside, but thanks to Tutor Iceflame's hard work, there was no sign of it in her beautifully set shoulders. The worst had happened: she could face it now that she had had time to prepare herself. "We'll fight."

"No," protested Padraig. "We've more important fish to fry, think on."

"There's nothing more important than ridding Llassar of the Fae," Dion said. "We fight."

"You have another purpose," said Barric. Dion met his eyes, seeing in their black depths the *life given in binding*, and knew that she would be too busy collecting shards of the Broken Sword to have any time left for leading an army.

"All right," she said. "But where do we begin?"

"And who *will* lead the fight?" demanded Aerwn, by no means pleased. She always hated to see Dion give way to anyone but herself. "We can't let Owain have all the fun! We're meant to meet him outside Tywyn."

Dion said: "You'll lead the fight, of course. You're second to the throne. When I die–"

"Nothing is going to happen to you!" said Aerwn furiously.

Dion looked at Barric, then Padraig, her eyes wide with dismay. "You didn't tell her?"

"They told me some nonsense about giving your life in Binding," Aerwn said, hunching her shoulders. "It's rubbish. Good magic doesn't kill humans."

"It's not killing me," said Dion. "Not exactly. It's me giving myself."

"I won't have it! I won't! I'm coming with you!"

Dion said quietly: "You can't. Someone needs to lead the fight, and no one less than one of us can do it. Who will stand up to the king and queen without a princess to lead them?"

"*You* lead them, then! I'll do the binding!"

"You can't," said Dion. "You're not special enough."

Aerwn choked on an involuntary laugh and tried to hide it in a dignified cough. "I'm *very* special, thank you! What can you do that I can't?"

"Magic," said Dion. "It's no use, Aer– we have to do what we have to do. I can't lead an army, but I can Bind the land. Besides, if we fail you'll need to take back Llassar by force."

Aerwn, silenced, sat back with her breakfast. She ate in silence for a few minutes before saying: "It's just me and the gingery old Duc, then, is it? All right. We're all of us for Tywyn, then?"

"Aye," said Padraig. He looked as if he had given up protesting about discussion over breakfast. "To begin with."

Aerwn grunted. "Well, I suppose that's *something*, anyway. I'll stay with you as long as I can. If you're going to go off and die I want to see as much of you as I can before you go."

Padraig batted his eyelashes at her. "Aye, I knew you cared!"

"You can die in a ditch as far as I'm concerned," Aerwn said politely. "If I'm only going to have my sister for another day, I'm not sharing."

Padraig winked at Dion. "Sure, we'll let Dion decide. A man of my good favour, or a lass of–"

"Careful," Aerwn warned, grinning broadly. "Dion and I look exactly the same."

"Not exactly," said Padraig. His eyes flicked briefly over Aerwn's head as he said to Barric: "Guests, big man."

Dion followed his gaze and saw a strange Fae by the edge of their camp, followed closely by a human woman. She gasped and hurled a fiery bolt of magic, her breakfast dish clattering to the rocky floor. The strange Fae caught her assault with a yell, and there was the scent of singeing.

Aerwn, instinctively covering her head, yelped: "Dion! Stop!"

"He's Fae!"

"He's on our side!"

Dion said: "N-none of them are on our side! Get away from him, Aerwn!"

"How appallingly rude!" said the Fae, wringing his scorched fingers. He cautiously felt his face and said in dismay: "My eyebrows! My luscious eyebrows!"

"Your eyebrows are fine," said the woman next to him. "Carmine, we've *talked* about you being so caught with your appearance."

"Yes, but that's when I'm being effortlessly gorgeous!" he protested.

"You're getting slow, Carmine," said Barric. "Peace, Dion."

Dion, who had been building another deadly charge of magic, very slowly let it dissipate. Carmine had been watching her cautiously, despite his loud dismay, and when the last of the magic left her fingers he relaxed again.

"Is this a new way of greeting friends?"

"Sorry," said Aerwn. "Di doesn't understand. She had a nasty experience or two with the Fae in Bithywis."

"Why are we working with Fae?" said Dion tightly. The anger that had been slowly building in her since that day in Bithywis was threatening to make her voice tremble, and she was by no means willing to trust any Fae, even if Barric and Aerwn *did* know him.

Aerwn tossed a frown back at her. "Sorry, what? You do know

that Padraig is Fae, too?" Padraig made a sharp noise of protest but Aerwn shot him a glare, too. "What? Why didn't you tell her? What were you playing at in Bithywis? And Barric–"

"*Peace*, Aerwn," said Barric. Aerwn turned resentful eyes on him but closed her mouth. "We have no time for talking. Finish your breakfast: we move in a quarter hour."

IT WAS BITTERLY cold for the time of year, thought Dion. The years had successively become colder since she was a child, which now seemed sinister somewhere at the back of her mind where all her private musings happened; but the last two years had been exponentially colder than those before. The summer sun that should have been warm on her head was thin and glittering, more beautiful than useful for warmth. Adding to the frozen feeling of the day was the chilly, uncomfortable knowledge that Padraig was walking beside her still, hours after they had left the environs of Harlech by stealth. He had tried to talk to her at first, his lively blue eyes unusually shadowed, but Dion had refused to answer his conversational gambits or even to look at him more than fleetingly. The trust that had grown between them as they journeyed toward Harlech was forgotten; and having learnt to hate the Fae in so short a time, she found herself unwilling to trust again so swiftly. Before long Padraig ceased trying to talk to her, but he didn't leave her side. Their silence was no match for the chatter from the Fae and the human girl up ahead, or for Aerwn's cheerful, if one-sided, conversation with Barric. Despite her declaration of wanting Dion all to herself, Aerwn had been keeping her distance. She looked slightly ashamed of herself.

Dion wished Padraig would walk with someone else; wished she didn't flush when she felt his eyes on her; wished above all that he wasn't *Fae*. The Fae were the enemy– *all* Fae were the enemy. How could their expedition be successful if there were two Fae in the company? How could she be certain that they wouldn't be betrayed?

Dion remained deep in thought as the morning drew out into afternoon, and then as the afternoon lengthened into evening. After they stopped for lunch her silence was less noticeable: everybody but Barric was also weary and silent, and Barric didn't speak a great deal at the best of times. Much to Dion's relief, he ousted Padraig from his position by her side some time before the sun began to go down, and she was able to take comfort in his tall, striding silence. If she had looked behind at Aerwn and Padraig, who were thus forced to walk side by side, she would have seen the angry looks they exchanged.

By the time the sun was setting they had begun to walk through light forest, and the last town was some hours behind them; now merely a flickering light on the horizon. Dion found herself curious: what were they doing at the base of the Caerphilly ranges? Tywyn was close, but south-easterly of their position. Were they to cross the ranges after Aerwn left them? Even in summer it would be a cold, arduous climb to cross them, and since it wasn't likely that they could take the king's highway through the mountains it would be a more arduous climb still. And then what? wondered Dion. The mountain scaled and descended, they would be in Shinpo; where the king and queen had reportedly been ousted from their throne and the land overrun by the Fae. Dion couldn't think of a worse place to begin their search for the shards– unless– unless Aerwn and Barric knew something that she didn't. That was likely to be the case, she thought rather wearily.

She said to Barric: "Does Aerwn know where the next shard is?" and found that her voice was rusty and cracking from lack of speaking.

"Aerwn!" called Barric, by way of reply. "Give me the shard." Something sharp and metallic hissed through the air at his head, and he caught it delicately between his fingers. "Here," he said, passing it to Dion. "See for yourself."

Dion took it gingerly, very much aware that she was holding her life in her hands, as it were, and as she held it she began to understand something of the certainty of their direction. The shard was unmistakeably pulling at her, drawing her towards north-east Shinpo in general and somewhere else in particular. She looked back up at Barric in wonder.

"It's– is it telling us where the other shards are?"

He nodded. "The closest one."

"But–" Dion stopped, unsure of how to voice what she was thinking without sounding either snide or ignorant.

"Why haven't we collected them earlier?" asked Padraig's voice. He and Aerwn had caught up with Dion and Barric while they were engaged and unheeding, and there was something of a determined look to his eyes. "Well, cherry, there was a difficulty. We Fae have an inbuilt disadvantage when it comes to the Broken Sword."

Dion's eyes flickered at him and then away. She said stiffly: "What disadvantage?"

"It's the nature of the thing. The Broken Sword is a defence against Faery–"

"Not against," said Barric. "Around."

"Even so," shrugged Padraig. "Yet the Fae are the ones most likely to challenge it, and the magic of the Sword reflects that. When we hold the shards, they tell us nothing. Nor are they comfortable for us to be around."

"*I* said we should begin collecting them earlier," said Aerwn. "I was wrong, actually. If we'd started collecting them earlier and tried to keep them safe ourselves, the Fae would probably already have them. I had to steal this one back as it was. Just think if I'd tried to give them to our parents."

Dion shared an identical grimace with her, and tried to give the shard back.

"No thanks," said Aerwn, and added frankly: "I've had enough of that thing. It's yours now: I'm not special enough, remember?"

THE CAMP WAS an uncomfortable place that night. Barric called a halt a little after darkness fell, and though they had a fire it didn't quite take the chill from the air. Padraig didn't try to sit with Dion, much to her relief: he threw himself down beneath a tree beside Aerwn, his eyes glittering in the firelight. Neither of them talked, but they both seemed to prefer it. It occurred to Dion that they may have been quarrelling about her, and she found that she could still feel guilty about it. She herself sat down beside Barric, warming herself against his huge side while he cleaned his throwing knives. The human woman who had come with Carmine—her name was Fancy, though her plain, sensible face didn't suit it—was cleaning her own blades, long and curved and deadly in the firelight. Both of them were not only preparing for, but *expecting*, a fight.

Across the fire she felt Padraig's eyes on her more often than not, and tried to ignore it by asking Barric: "Why is Carmine on first watch?" She saw his eyes flick up briefly to her face, and flushed. "We can't trust the Fae."

Barric nodded, observing the edge of one of his knives closely. "And all humans are for humankind."

"They–" Dion bit her lip. She knew, and *Barric* knew, that Dion couldn't help but think of her parents. She said grittily: "They *should* be."

There was a steady, thoughtful silence while Barric buffed another knife clean and put it down carefully on the grass. Then he said: "Coinnach was Fae: Padraig's Unseelie bloodline was named in prophecy."

Dion turned one of his knives between her fingers. "Why does the prophecy call for Fae help to defeat Faery? Why would they help?"

"Why do you help?"

"I'm human, of course," said Dion, very much surprised.

"And Alawn's daughter," Barric reminded her. "You weren't loyal to your family."

"Because my family was *wrong*."

"Ah," said Barric again. "You think Fae have no consciences. Do you think Padraig has no conscience?"

"He– yes. Yes, he does." Dion knew he did. She would have sworn that his anger at the Fae in Bithywis was entirely real. Once again, all that she knew to be true and right was swinging wildly.

"Do you doubt that he will reforge the Sword?"

"I don't know," she said, leaning into his side tiredly. "Barric, I don't know anything anymore. Everything I thought I knew was wrong and now I don't know what to believe."

Barric shifted until one of his arms was comfortably around her and used Dion's hands to polish the knife she was still holding. "Do you believe me?"

"You're the only one I *do* still believe," said Dion, her eyes falling on Aerwn. Her sister would be leaving tomorrow and Dion still had no idea what to say to her. "How is it that I couldn't tell Padraig was Fae? He looked—he *looks*—human."

"Padraig has grown up knowing his place in the prophecy: he sublimated his magic to serve it."

"It's all in the hammer and anvil," said Dion, closing her eyes briefly. She was gallingly annoyed with herself for not having realised as much. The magic in the hammer and anvil was, as she had said to Padraig at the time, Fae. If she had looked closer at the tiny spark of magic that remained within him– but it was just one more thing to add to the list of Things Dion Was Too Blind and Ignorant To See.

Barric said: "Mind the edge, Dion. There: your finger is bleeding." He took the knife from her, wiping the trickle of blood onto the grass, and brushed over her thumb with his own much larger one, smoothing a gleam of golden magic into it. "You'll know that sort of magic again by the destiny-thread."

Interested in spite of herself, Dion said: "It *was* a destiny thread! I thought so!"

Barric nodded. "Your own will be used in the binding of the sword."

"I know."

"You're not so different." Dion opened her mouth to reply but caught Barric's eye and found that she couldn't. "He's as much a part of this as you are."

"He's *Fae*." It was sickening how often it came back to that one point: that one, impossible point.

"As am I," he said. "Will you hate me, too?"

Dion froze in shock, her eyes flying up to meet Barric's. "I don't– I wouldn't! I know you. I love you. But how can you be Fae? Your magic is all wrong. You have an iron greatsword!"

"I'm a Guardian," he said. "Fae stock with a different strain of magic. Iron has no power over us."

"Why didn't–" Dion began, and then flushed. "I wouldn't have listened to you if you'd told me you were a Guardian. I'd have called the Fae in. Oh, Barric, this is such a mess!"

Barric tapped one knife against his boot and abandoned it on the grass, unpolished. "There's nothing messy about it," he said. "I'm Fae. Padraig's Fae. Our kind is just as likely to be bad or good as your kind. You'll accept it or you won't."

Dion let her gaze linger on Padraig. In Bithywis, she had liked him. There was a kind of honesty about him that appealed to her despite the fact that it disconcerted her to the point of blushing and stuttering. She never quite knew what he would say or do next. As they travelled on to Harlech it had occurred to her more than once that Padraig was someone she could even love, given enough time to get to know him. Padraig didn't seem to under-stand the concept of slow and steady, and Dion had been as often frightened back into her shell as charmed out of it, but she'd been surprised at how happy she was to see him again that morning. Barric, as unpleasant as it was to consider it, was right. Padraig hadn't changed: he was as he had ever been. It was Dion's own perception that had changed. In mulling it over, she gazed at Padraig just an instant too long; and he turned his head and caught her at it. He gave her a warm, brilliant smile with no reserve to it at all, and Dion found a smile tugging at her own lips. She saw him shift his hands as if to push himself up and dropped her eyes at once. She wanted to sleep on her thoughts and she knew she wouldn't be able to think clearly if Padraig was sitting beside her and whispering in her ear. She let her eyes flutter up again briefly and found that he had settled back down beneath his tree. He was still smiling, and his eyes glowed like sapphires. He held her eyes for a moment longer, then closed his own and appeared to go to sleep.

Dion looked up at Barric, who was methodically sliding his knives back into their sheaths within his clothes, and felt a light, dizzying relief. "Barric," she said. "I said before that I love you."

Barric's hands grew still, a knife half-sheathed. "Yes?"

"Well, it's not true," she said, wrapping her arms as far as they would go around his massive torso. "I love you *very* much."

The knife snicked home, and one large arm enfolded her briefly, obscuring the light-speckled darkness of the sky with the softer darkness of Barric's ebony skin. She felt him drop a kiss on the top of her head and tilted her head to smile up at him.

He smiled back at her, his scar ruching his cheek, and said: "Your sister wants to talk to you." He rose silently, vacating his seat for Aerwn, and crossed the camp softly to speak with Fancy.

"Oh, good!" said Aerwn, throwing herself down beside Dion. "You've finished thinking it through. I *told* Padraig it wouldn't take you long; he's been out of sorts and annoying all day. Now that *that*'s over, can we talk about something else?"

"You're the one who started talking about him!" protested Dion, laughing.

"Don't know what you're talking about," said Aerwn, wriggling into a more comfortable position with much elbowing and shoving. "Here, snuggle under my cloak. We're going to talk all night."

DION WOKE EARLY OR LATE, she wasn't sure which. Despite Aerwn's threat, they hadn't talked *all night*; or even half the night. They had fallen asleep in each other's arms for the first time in years, from which position Dion extricated herself with great difficulty and a sore neck. She stretched and tried to massage the pinch from her neck, finding herself refreshed and unwilling to lie back down. It was a beautiful night: there was no sign of either sunrise or sunset, and the moon was bright in the sky. Carmine was standing—or rather, sitting—guard; stretched out beneath the tree whose roots curled around the slumbering Fancy, his arms folded and his booted feet crossed at the ankle. One of his hands rested on Fancy's head. He nodded at Dion as she rose and left camp, quietly making her way across the leaf-strewn forest floor. Perhaps he thought she was visiting the latrine Aerwn had dug behind one of the trees.

It was very cold beneath the trees. Dion thought she sensed an alien brittleness to the night, and wondered for the first time if the Fae had brought more than death and destruction with them when they left Faery for the human world. Here in Llassar where the Seelie Fae were more prevalent, the days had lengthened and the nights seemed brighter, if less alive. Did Illisr, with its huge population of Unseelie, find its days shorter and darker to suit the night Fae? And if so, what other physical changes had the Fae brought with them? She didn't dare wander too far, fearful of losing the camp even in the bright moonshine, but there was a pleasant rock overlooking a silvery, moon-bathed gully nearby, and Dion settled herself quietly there. Something was niggling at the back of her mind, and it wasn't until she was able to sit down and think about it that she realised it was the shard. It was in her pocket, prickling at her consciousness with the knowledge that somewhere out there in the general direction of Shinpo, a shard just like it was moving closer to her. Or, thought Dion, frowning in confusion, *was* it? First the other shard seemed to tug at her mind from Shinpo, then she seemed to feel a tug from the south-east, on the Llassarian side of the border. Which was it? North-east, beyond the border, or south-east and within?

"You should be sleeping, cherry," said Padraig's voice. Dion jumped and nearly lost her shard in the darkness of the night. While she was fumbling for it, Padraig leapt lightly up on the rock and sat down beside her, close enough to feel his warmth without quite touching her. "We're in for a hard march tomorrow, sure. Aerwn and ap Rees will buy some time, but not enough for us to dawdle about our business."

"I'll go back soon," said Dion. She added quietly, without quite meaning to: "You should have told me yourself."

"Aye," said Padraig. "Aye, and so I knew."

"Then *why–*"

"Pure self-interest," he said. "I didn't wish for you to think badly of me. And how could I blame you for it? There's barely a man of the Fae that I'd trust, myself."

When Dion had time to think it over later, she would come to realise that this very moment was the moment she fell in love with Padraig, in all his honest dishonesty. She had no time to think about it at that point, however, because exactly at that moment, Aerwn screamed. Padraig was up from the rock in an instant, catching Dion around the waist as she tried to dash headlong through the trees and back to camp.

"Can you fight, cherry?"

"Yes," said Dion; and then, as she heard the unmistakable sound of metal battering metal in the clash of swords: "No. Not that kind."

"Then stay behind me and use whatever magic springs to mind. *Quietly* now: we'll likely need all the advantage we can get."

Dion, used to subduing her own wishes to the greater good, had never found it so hard to concede. Their swift, silent passage back to camp seemed to stretch into an eternity– an eternity where she didn't hear another sound from Aerwn, only the ugly striking of sword against sword. Dion wasn't quite sure if she was panting or sobbing by the time they were within sight of the camp. In the low firelight she could see a tableau stained red: Fancy, a dancing, beautiful creature of sharp edges and deadly curves, her blades singing through the air too quickly to follow; Barric, a wall of certain death, his greatsword cutting through the knot of Fae that surrounded him as he forged his way slowly forward to Aerwn, who was pinned beneath three other Fae and still struggling furiously. Carmine had vanished from sight.

Dion, unpleasantly weak at the knees and already shaking, would have started into the battle in spite of all if Padraig hadn't said, still more insistently: "Wait, cherry. They're not trying to kill us; they're trying to capture us. See how they try to herd the big man? They've laid a snare somewhere for him. Stay here and don't give yourself away: I'll try to swing the tide for us. We can't afford to lose you by accident."

"We can't afford to lose you, either," protested Dion, but Padraig was already gone. She turned her fearful attention back to the shifting fight and saw Padraig join it, his hammer beating a path through Fae. She sent a simple spell or two slithering into the melee, hoping to slow down the mob around Barric, but each of them sank into static as they met armour laced with the same kind of sloughing spell she had made for Aerwn. Dion tried again with an even simpler spell to make the grass catch at enemy feet, but after Padraig twice stumbled as well she didn't dare to attempt another.

Instead, she had to endure the sight of the skirmish turning against her friends, the taste of bile in her mouth. Dion sank to her knees, her breath too fast, and tried desperately to think of another form of attack. It was already too late, she knew: many Fae had fallen, but many more still were dogging Barric, Fancy, and Padraig. Aerwn was already out of it, and if she had to guess Dion would have said that the lumpy roll next to her sister was a bound and gagged Carmine. Barric was forced back inch by inch until something magical and sharp snapped, hoisting him above the fight in a bundle of tight, unbreakable cords. A shout went up from the Fae, and Padraig and Fancy disappeared beneath a surge of enemy Fae almost immediately. Dion, at first too terrified for Padraig even to weep, saw him appear again, bundled as tightly as Barric but alive, and let the tears fall thankfully down her cheeks. Padraig was right. These Fae wanted captives, not dead men.

Dion expected that the Fae, having obtained their prey, would camp for the night. They did no such thing. Instead, they heaved their captives between them, two to a person—or in Barric's case, four—and set out into the moonlit night with very little pause. It was perhaps natural: they were all Unseelie Fae, and darkness and moonlight were their delight. Dion, following along behind and wincing at every twig that broke beneath her feet, found that they were heading higher into the Caerphilly Ranges. At least, she thought, oddly amused amidst the sickness of dread that she felt; at least they were being taken in the right direction. Only Aerwn would be put out to have to travel so far back. She could still feel the other shard nearby, tugging at her own, and knew they were heading in the right direction.

The Fae marched until dawn began to spill pink and orange light across their pale faces. During the night they had crested the mountain at its lowest point, the Llassarian forest giving way to rock and patches of rich green grass, and Dion had had to fall back in order not to be seen. Through the chill of first morning until the glimmering of dawn, she followed the Fae down the mountainside and into Shinpo, creeping from rock-face to rock-face. Further down the mountain she could see the patchy rock overgrown by jungle; gradually at first, in a riot of vines, and then in a crowding of lush foliage.

At last, just as Dion began to think that the Fae would never stop, their leader looked around at the pinky-peach dawn in disfavour and called a halt. They swiftly set up camp, and she felt her heart sink a little more. The camp was so open that she would be seen by any watch they chose to set up before she got within a quarter mile of it. She had been hoping to sneak in while they slept, but with such bright dawn and sparseness of cover it was impossible. If only they had set up camp a little closer to the Shinpoan jungle! Dion tucked herself close to a cool rock-face with the grass soft beneath her, weary and beaten; and since she could do nothing else, followed the example of the Fae, and went to sleep.

She woke to the unsatisfactory brightness of noon sunlight on her face. Despite its brightness it didn't warm her, and she shivered as she sat up. To her relief, the Fae camp was still there when she popped her head around the rock-face to catch a glimpse of it. Her shard was almost burning against her leg through its pocket, surprising Dion at how much closer the other shard had gotten while she slept. There was no time to wonder about it, however: the closer to twilight it was before she made her move, the less likely it was that she would succeed. Approaching the camp herself was still out of the question: even if she hid herself with magic, it was unlikely that a Fae lookout wouldn't be trained to see through it. And she already knew that any spells she threw at them would simply slide off.

All right, thought Dion, ripping up grass as she mused; then suppose she thought like Ywain, with his strategically-placed piles of bricks. Only instead of confusing the eye with something that was arranged by magic but not technically a spell, she would attack the soldiers with something affected by magic but not inherently magic itself. Let their spells try to slough off grass that sank beneath them like quicksand, or rocks that hungrily seized their ankles– or even, thought Dion with a narrow-eyed look at the dense foliage that began further down the mountain, vines that constricted their arms to their sides and dragged them back into the darkness of Shinpoan jungle. She drew a deep breath, her fingers sinking into the grass beneath her, and brought the land around her to malicious life.

Dion heard the screams from the Fae camp as if from a vast distance, and ignored them. She was in the vines and the rocks and the sinking earth beneath, desperately trying to make sure that there were pockets of safety around her companions while Fae screamed and ran. And somewhere overhead—whether in the camp or where Dion actually sat, she wasn't quite sure—a dragon soared.

That's just ridiculous, she thought. *I didn't make a dragon.* But it was there all the same, plucking Fae soldiers from her vines in order to tear their heads from their bodies, and swooping in on the ones who had been quick enough to discover the safety of remaining near the prisoners. Dion distantly felt the impact of a body nearby and heard a female voice yell: "Hey! Watch where you're throwing those things!"

Then the same female voice said in her ear: "You might as well stop now. Rafiq will take care of the rest of them. They tried to kill me two days ago and he's been a bit annoyed about it ever since."

Dion released her grip on the land and let herself become smaller, weaker; exhausted. There was a Shinpoan girl crouching beside her, neck-scarf pinned tightly against the wind and her almond eyes bright with friendly interest. Her mouth was pulled up on one side by a small scar as much as by her smile, and nearly every bit of bare skin that showed was similarly marred. Even Barric wasn't so scarred.

Dion, trying to gather her thoughts into reasonable order, said: "Is that your dragon?"

"That's one way of putting it," said the girl.

"Oh, good," said Dion. "I didn't think I'd conjured one. I should go and get my friends: they weren't expecting a dragon."

"No one ever really expects a dragon," said the girl, offering a hand to help Dion up. "That's kind of the point."

"Thanks for helping," said Dion, with a shy smile. She could feel her shard resting against her leg, searingly hot: the other girl was also carrying a shard. She didn't mention it, but Dion knew that she must know Dion had one, too. The dragon explained why it had been moving so swiftly toward them.

"Oh, well; it's good for Rafiq to get it all out of his system," said the other girl. She added: "Your friends must have been waiting for a distraction."

She was gazing ahead, and Dion, following her eyes, saw Barric and Fancy busily untying the others. When Barric saw them approaching he dropped Aerwn back on the grass, much to her shrill indignation, and strode across the rocky mountainside to scoop up Dion.

"Huh. I should get myself one of those," said the other girl, trotting a bit to keep up with Barric's long stride. "Very handy over rough terrain."

Dion giggled; and, finding herself inclined to rebel, said to Barric: "I can walk."

"I know," he said, without even the smallest suggestion of slowing down or stopping. "But it was a beautiful piece of working and you should be resting."

By the time they were a stone's throw away, Fancy had untied the others, and Padraig was hurrying to meet them. Kako looked up at Dion with one brow lifted, and Dion found herself blushing.

"A day's walk!" Aerwn was saying, when they approached. "Another *whole day*'s walk! It's all right for you lot: you're exactly where you want to be. I'm the only one who has to backtrack."

"Best get started, then, hadn't you?" said Padraig unsympathetically. Aerwn glared at him, and Dion thought that things were about to disintegrate into a childish quarrel when the dragon swooped in close and landed rather too near for comfort.

Fancy's knives were back out in an instant, as was Padraig's hammer. The girl stepped away from Barric and Dion, putting herself between their weapons and her dragon, her hands spread wide. "We can stand here pointing weapons at each other," she said. "Or we can get on with discussing exactly what we plan to do with the shards."

There was an immediate babble of noise: most of it from Padraig and Carmine, with an occasional, slightly sarcastic comment from the girl. She didn't seem to be particularly intimidated, even by Barric. That could have been because of her dragon, but Dion didn't think so. At last, she said amiably: "Oh, shut up, you two," at Padraig and Carmine, and said to Dion: "You're the shard-holder, aren't you?"

Dion threw a quick look up at Barric, but his face was impassive, so she said: "Yes. Barric, put me down, *please.*"

Barric's scar pulled, but he put her down. She found herself less steady than she would have liked, and kept a tight grip on his arm as she said to Kako: "You've been looking for us. Why?"

"I have my own shard, of course. We've been trying to piece the Broken Sword back together. Rafiq and I had to leave home in rather a hurry: the Fae got impatient and took over the castle in Shinpo. We weren't expecting it. We thought we had a bit more time before things got so dangerous."

Padraig, his hammer dropping to his side, said in dismay: "We'd heard that the castle had been taken. I was hoping it was an exaggeration."

"It wasn't," said the girl. There was sorrow in her eyes, deep and unresolved. "We were cut off when it fell."

"Cut off," said Barric slowly. "Who are you?"

"I'm Kako," the girl said. She looked up over her shoulder as if sharing a joke with the dragon behind her. "This is Rafiq."

Much to Dion's surprise, Barric bowed deeply. Kako looked at first surprised, and then very much amused. Barric said: "I'm sorry to hear of your parents. Are your brother and sisters–"

"Don't know," said Kako lightly. There was the barest tremble in her voice, and Dion knew with a searing sense of fellowship that the other girl was only just holding back tears. "We weren't able establish any kind of communication."

The dragon shifted forward, startling Carmine and Fancy into a hasty retreat, and dipped his huge head to breathe a small huff of smoke into Kako's hair. She patted his head absently and looked relieved when Dion said: "How did you get your shard?"

"A fortunate coincidence," said Kako, wrapping her arm around Rafiq's nose. "It seems to work like that with the shards. It's almost like *they* find *you* instead of the other way around."

"I'm more interested in knowing how you know about the Broken Sword," said Padraig, his blue eyes watchful. "There were two copies of *The Song of the Broken Sword*: one is destroyed and the other is still in Avernse."

"Yes, but I have a dragon," said Kako. "I might as well wonder why *you* know about it, if we're going to be suspicious of each other."

"I'm Fae," said Padraig, his nose flaring.

"Exactly," Kako said. "*Very* suspicious. There's no use looking for reasons to mistrust each other; we might as well just get on with it. There's at least one more shard in Shinpo and another in Montalier. That makes four, and Rafiq says there's only seven of them."

"Five," said Dion absently. It had occurred to her that there was still a discrepancy in the position of Kako's shard: she knew it to be just a few feet away with Kako, but she could still feel the tug of her own that said another shard was nearby. So close nearby, in fact, that she added: "There's another shard here."

"That?" said Kako, looking surprised. "I thought that was just an echo sort of effect that your shard was giving off."

"So did I," Dion said. "I'm not so sure, now." She made her

way rather waveringly toward what had been the outer edge of the Fae camp with Kako beside her, their eyes scanning the grass.

"Oh, here we go!" said Kako, poking at a headless corpse with one foot. "This one's got it."

"They can't have been tracking us with it," Dion said, frowning. She knelt by the body, wincing as she went through its pockets. "So why have it?"

"I've got a theory about that," said Kako, briskly going through the pockets on the other side of the body with considerably more relish and considerably less wincing. "It's like I said before: the shards seem to find us instead of the other way around. He might not even have known what he had."

"Maybe," said Dion uneasily. "Oh! I've got it!"

"Oh," said Kako, sounding disappointed. "I suppose that means it's yours, then."

Dion snuffled a laugh. "We should probably keep them separate, anyway. If we're attacked again at least one of us should be able to get away. Barric can look after this one."

Barric, already silently waiting beside her, took it without complaint. He said: "Have you got a bearing on the next shard?"

"*Much* better!" said Kako. She glanced at Dion. "North-westerly Shinpo? Maybe one in Illisr as well."

Dion said in relief: "Yes. And something further on in Montalier."

"We'd best be moving, then," said Barric. "Aerwn, do you know your way?"

"Yes," said Aerwn. "But I'm going to miss my set time with Owain. Hopefully he'll wait for me."

"You can fly," said Kako to her, unexpectedly. "No need for walking two days when you can fly a few hours instead."

"I'll take too long, sure," said Padraig. "You're a bonny fighter, Aerwn, but yourself and ap Rees can only stand against the Fae for so long. By the time we've foot-marched all the way to

Montalier and back again you'll be dead or worse. Much better that the dragon comes with us."

"Thanks a lot," said Aerwn, grinning.

"We don't need to get back," said Dion. "Once we have the shards and the sword is remade, we only have to travel on to Avernse to find the place where the Sword originally bound Faery. You can hold out until then, can't they?"

"Aerwn and ap Rees are capable," said Barric with finality.

"We don't need to walk," Kako said. She said it as if it should be obvious. "We'll fly, too, of course."

There was a rather uncomfortable silence. Dion wasn't sure if it was because Rafiq looked both distinctly dangerous and distinctly hungry, or if it was because of the fact that there simply weren't enough dragons to send in both directions.

"Unless you've got another dragon up those sleeves of yours," remarked Carmine, speaking the thoughts of everyone else, "it seems unlikely that we'll all fit."

"Not exactly up my sleeve," said Kako, with a secret smile. "Please don't panic, everyone. I'm about to show you a new trick I've learned."

Dion somehow wasn't very surprised when Kako began to grow, scales rippling across her skin and colour blooming. A heart-beat later, a second dragon was coiled on the grass cover beside Rafiq, her head butting against his shoulder in friendly greeting. By dragonish standards she was small, compact, and well-shaped: Dion wasn't surprised to see the delicate flourish of colour to Rafiq's scales that, if she had correctly learned her dragon emotions, meant he was fully aware of Kako's charms. By human standards Kako was dauntingly large: she dwarfed even Barric completely.

Aerwn, her eyes shining, said: "I take it back. I'm glad we were captured."

"Me too," said Fancy, her eyes just as wide as Aerwn's. "How *beautiful!* I'd heard that some dragons could take human form, but I've never seen it!"

I'm not exactly a dragon, said a familiar voice. It buzzed in Dion's ears in an illusion of sound. *I'm more of a human who can take dragon form. I've had to practise a lot: I've only just learned how to do it properly. Rafiq is the real dragon.*

You take the curly-haired one, said another large, thrumming voice. *I'll take the others.*

"I want to go with Aerwn," said Dion. There was an immediate outcry.

"You *can't*, Di! What if we're captured?"

Padraig said: "Aye, let's not make a division of ourselves. Cherry, you're the most important one of us. We can't risk losing you."

"Too risky," agreed Fancy. "And we are in a hurry, after all. If you go one way and we go another–"

Barric, his dark eyes thoughtful, said nothing at all.

"I'm just as likely to be captured with one dragon as with another," said Dion resolutely.

"Which is to say, not likely at all," remarked Aerwn, only half-convinced. "It's not that I don't want you, Di; but Fancy's right. The quicker you find the shards, the better it'll go for Owain and me."

"I can catch everyone up when they stop for the night," Dion objected. "The next shard is at least a day away yet, even if we are flying. I'm not going to see you again and I want to make sure you get safely back to Llassar."

I'm the faster flier, said Kako. *If that helps.*

"I'll go with them," said Barric briefly. "Padraig, Fancy, Carmine– go with Rafiq. Do you have a familiar meeting place?"

Outside Lo'him, said Rafiq. *There's a cattle-shed we've used before.*

"That must be an impressive cattle-shed," said Carmine, observing the two dragons with one eyebrow up.

Padraig looked as though he would have liked to protest, but Barric was already boosting Dion and Aerwn up on Kako's silvery-blue back. Dion, laughing at a rueful grimace from Padraig, saw the habitual glitter of amusement wake in his eyes, and the elaborate bow he gave as Barric swung himself into place behind her. Kako leapt into flight almost immediately after that, and Dion was too busy gasping for breath to do more than grip tightly to Barric's arms and hope rather wildly that she wasn't going to disgrace herself by throwing up on Kako's beautiful scales.

Once the uneven takeoff was out of the way, flying was surprisingly enjoyable. Dion and Aerwn shouted to each other over the wail of the wind and the flap of Kako's wings as if they were out on horseback, enjoying the summer afternoon. They didn't talk about war, or binding, or even the Fae: Dion, leaning forward with her arms around Aerwn's waist, eagerly pointed out familiar landmarks and sights, both of them kept from slipping to certain death by Barric's watchfulness. Kako shamelessly eavesdropped, interposing a comment every now and then and frankly interested when she discovered that Dion and Aerwn were the princesses of Llassar.

Even Dai didn't rebel to this extent, she said, her voice touched with amusement. *Mind you, Shinpo already has enough rebels as it is. I suppose that makes us sisters, according to my elder sister's theory on the Sisterhood of Princesses. I'm the third princess of Shinpo– or what's left of it, anyway.*

That explained the sorrow in her eyes when she spoke of the fall of the castle, thought Dion, with a stab of sadness. The conversation faltered after that, and it wasn't long before they landed in a convenient pasture close to Tywyn, scattering cattle every which way. Barric and Kako stayed where they were by unspoken agreement, while Dion walked Aerwn to the edge of the field.

"Are you sure we're in the right place?" She hadn't seen any sign of an army—be it rag-tag citizenry *or* well-drilled troops—and she had the worried feeling that she should have.

Aerwn nodded. "I saw Owain's signal as we cleared the last field. He'll already be looking for me. The others are meant to be laying low in Tywyn and camping out in a few friendly barns. By the end of the week we'll have too many to hide in barns, though."

"Aerwn–" Dion stopped, and then said: "I'm sorry we weren't so close for the last few years."

"My fault," said Aerwn, her voice short and clipped. Dion wasn't fooled: Aerwn didn't like to be seen as anything other than strong, and the closer she was to tears, the terser she became. "We'll fight as long as we can. Try not to let them kill us."

"I'll do my best," Dion said, smiling just as brightly as Aerwn. She hugged her sister to escape the necessity of keeping up the facade, and felt Aerwn's arms fairly crush her ribcage.

"I love you," said Aerwn. "I didn't want to be queen, Di."

"I know," Dion said. "I love you, too."

Aerwn was still waving when she became too small for Dion to see. Dion leant back into Barric, sinking under the weight of exhaustion and sorrow, and was pulled closer.

"Go to sleep," he said. "We've a long way to go yet."

"I was promised a bath," said Carmine's voice. Dion could hear it carrying from the barn, where a soft glow of light spilled out on the grass to welcome them. Kako shot her a sarcastic grin as Carmine's voice added: "A *hot* bath. How can I be expected to maintain my impossibly high standard of personal beauty without the proper ablutionary requisites? I refuse to spend the night in straw, without even the hope of hot water."

They entered the barn in time to see Padraig grinning, and Dion even saw Barric's scar twitch slightly. Fancy rolled her eyes without taking pains to hide the fact.

"Fancy, what have I told you about rolling your eyes at me?" Carmine demanded.

"You said to keep doing it while you were in too much danger of becoming a prat."

"Oh," said Carmine. "Well, what sort of scale am I being judged by? Who decides how much danger I'm in?"

"I do," said Fancy. "You gave me permission."

"I don't remember this. When was all this decided?"

"One day after you were being more of a prat than usual," said Fancy. She nodded at Barric and the two girls, and it wasn't until the tall, dark-skinned man at her side shouldered his way past Dion to greet Kako that Dion realised there was another member of their party.

Rafiq, she realised, as Padraig said beside her: "A neat trick, is it not?"

"How wonderful!" said Dion, watching Rafiq and Kako critically. She wasn't sure if Kako was aware of it, but Rafiq as a human male was even more possessive and watchful than Rafiq as a dragon had been.

"They could hardly be better matched, could they?" murmured Padraig.

"No," Dion said, much amused. She thought Kako was quite intelligent, and it surprised her to see that the girl had no idea of her dragon's attachment to her. "A dragon who can transform into a human, and a human who can transform into a dragon. What are the odds of such a beautifully matched pair meeting?"

Padraig gave her a very deliberate wink. "Oh, better than you think, cherry, sure!"

"What was Carmine complaining about?" Dion asked, flushing pink. "We could hear him across the yard."

"Rafiq said there would be hot baths and real food when we got to Lo'him," said Padraig, accepting the change in subject with only the smallest smile hovering on his lips. "Carmine was expressing his dissatisfaction with having to wait for the three of you."

"Oh, is that what it was?" said Kako, sauntering in their direction. Rafiq followed her closely, his stride just a little too stilted. "Well, we'd better get a move on, then. We can walk from here: there's a nice place in Lo'him where we can get food and beds...and hot baths," she added, for Carmine's benefit.

"Should we–" Dion started, then stopped. She didn't really expect anyone to pay attention, but both Barric and Padraig were looking at her expectantly, and Kako said: "Go on, then."

"Well, I've just thought of something," she said slowly. "The shards are attracted to each other."

"I suspected so right away," said Carmine immediately.

Dion couldn't help smiling. "Yes, all right, we all know it. But I've been wondering if we should be staying somewhere that's as full of Fae as a Shinpoan town. That Fae back at the border– why did he have one of the shards? What if more of them have shards?"

"What if they do?" Padraig said. "I feel nothing when I hold the shard. The magic is not for Fae."

"No," said Kako, her dark eyes thoughtful. She exchanged a worried look with Dion. "But what if the Fae found out about it? They already know we're trying to collect the shards: it strikes me that it's a very handy way of finding out where we are. Or of predicting where we'll be."

"Let them come," said Rafiq, with a rather heated smile that alarmed Dion. "Fae are just as deliciously chewable as humans."

"Even if they did find out," said Fancy. "Would it matter? I mean, they'd know about it, but they couldn't use it. The shard wouldn't let them."

"I don't know," Dion said. "That's why I'm worried."

Barric's eyes flitted from Kako to Dion. "Has the next shard moved at all?"

"No," said Kako, while Dion shook her head.

"Then on to baths and beds," said Carmine firmly. "I refuse to spend a night in the straw for a threat that may not exist."

Barric hesitated, his eyes still on Dion. She, unwilling to annoy the rest of the company for a fear so unfounded, said quickly: "We might as well. Kako's right: the shard hasn't moved."

"Then we'd best be moving," said Barric, after another brief pause. "We've already lost the light. Will they let us in after dark?"

"They're used to us arriving at odd hours," said Kako cheerfully. "Send out that little glow-light of yours, Carmine. We're going to need it."

Dion was beginning to feel the dampness of a dewy morning by the time they found themselves on the rutted main road of Lo'him. She was feeling decidedly refreshed thanks to her dragon-back sleep, her mind far too busy with thoughts of Aerwn and the finding of the next shard to welcome the idea of sleep. Padraig wasn't so fortunate: his yawns were many and contagious, and even Barric was stifling a yawn while Kako bargained with an inn-keeper for the use of half the inn. As she had promised, the keeper didn't seem to find it unusual to receive guests in the early hours of the morning, and it wasn't long before they had commandeered a small common-room upstairs with a shared bathing chamber opening into it, one small dining room downstairs, and two double-rooms beside that.

Padraig said: "Looks like we'll be sharing," and wriggled his eyebrows at Dion. Barric bore him off by the neck like a recalcitrant puppy with barely a twitch of his scar, leaving Carmine to do his own eyebrow wriggling at Fancy until she shooed him away as well.

THERE WAS ALREADY breakfast laid out in the dining room when Dion rose the next morning. None of the other women were awake, so she left their bedroom quietly without doing more than dressing in her clothes from yesterday. Despite the earliness of the hour, someone had already cleaned them, and Dion was equally charmed to see the breakfast laid when she briefly put her head around the dining room door. She took her time in the washing chamber: it was small, but equipped with very decent magic-assisted plumbing, a pleasure she hadn't enjoyed since she left Harlech. Besides, it unlikely that anyone besides Barric would also be up this early to interrupt her. Secure in that knowledge, Dion was therefore very much surprised to find Padraig already in the dining room when she returned thither, her stomach growling.

"Top of the morning to you, cherry," he said, his chair propped on its two back legs. "I wouldn't be putting your pretty head out of doors this morning if I were you: the streets are crawling with Fae. It's a nasty sight this early in the morning, to be sure."

Dion, who had been helping herself liberally from one of the hot dishes, frowned. "Why? This is such a small town: I thought we'd manage to avoid that sort of thing until we were further into Shinpo."

"Aye, but it's near enough to the border," said Padraig. "Could be they've heard rumours of an uprising in Llassar and want to strengthen their borders."

"So long as they don't cross it to help the Fae in Llassar," Dion said, her breakfast losing all appeal.

"It'll not come to that," Padraig said comfortably, setting his chair back on all four legs. "Don't shake your curls at me, cherry. Shinpoan Fae may have nudged across the border to snabble us, but they're not likely to cross the border in numbers. If there's one thing I know, it's the Fae; selfish, inward-looking bunch that we are. We divide naturally into cantons and factions, each of us wanting to be lord of our own domain and unwilling to give way to the others. It's why we need the Guardians, think on. We none of us love them, but we do need them."

"The Guardians are a sort of *Watch*, then?" Dion said doubtfully. She would have sat down a few seats away if Padraig, leaning forward, hadn't tugged at the hem of her jerkin and made her sit down rather suddenly beside him, her plate tilting dangerously.

"No need to be stand-offish, cherry," he said, resting his arm along the back of her chair. "Aye, it could be said that the Guardians are a kind of Watch: they keep us from being too much at each other's throats and stop us when we step beyond our bounds. It's as if when the races were made, the Seelie and Unseelie were made for all uncaring lightness, and the Guardians all staidness and responsibility."

"Then why–" Dion stopped, aware that her question could be construed as ungrateful. Padraig raised his brows encouragingly, and she went on: "Then why is Barric the only one helping us?"

"That's the thing, now," said Padraig. "They're a small, lonely race, the Guardians. I know of no more than five of them: all big brutes like Barric, and mighty long-lived, even for Fae. They move in shadows and prophecy. No doubt they've been looking and planning and waiting for you ever since you were a gleam in your father's eye. They move mountains on the wing of the butterfly; here a little, there a little, always unseen until the whole crumbles all at once."

"That's *exactly* what it was like!" Dion said. "A flutter here and there, and suddenly, an avalanche." She ate in silence for a few minutes, very much aware of Padraig twining his fingers in the corkscrew ends of her curls; then turned her face toward him. "Do you ever wonder if you'll get it right? The reforging, I mean?"

"Oh, I know well enough what needs to be done," said Padraig, with a smile. "'Tis the simplest and most difficult thing in the world. What of you, cherry? Was the big man's teaching inadequate?"

"Of course not!"

"Softly, cherry," murmured Padraig, his eyes laughing at her.

"I'm not criticising the big man: it occurred to me that you're not so sure of your own part."

"I am," said Dion uncertainly; "and I'm not. Barric couldn't teach me exactly what to do because no one knows exactly what needs to be done."

"He's been turning up in your mirror for the last ten years to teach you nothing in particular? I fully understand the urge to keep visiting you, cherry, but that strikes me as a little odd."

"He didn't teach me *nothing*!" said Dion. She found that she had leaned forward in her indignation, and that Padraig was also leaning in, his lips curving. She sat back rather hurriedly. "He taught me magic. Not so much spells and workings, but magic itself. How it moves and behaves, how it joins together, and why it does what it does. He told me from the beginning that he wouldn't be able to teach me just what to do."

Padraig seemed to sober, but there was still a suggestion of laughter to his eyes. "What will you do?"

"I don't know," said Dion. "That's why I can't stop thinking about the Binding. What if I get it wrong?"

"Tell me something, cherry," Padraig said, leaning forward again. "For such a faunish little thing, I've not yet seen you shy away from the prophecy. Are you really not afraid to die?"

"That's the easy bit," said Dion, uncomfortable at the implied praise. "I don't have to worry about doing it the wrong way. I'm afraid of failing almost everything else, but I know I can do that. I'm not *brave*, Padraig: I never have been. I've been a coward for as long as I can remember."

"It's an odd thing," Padraig said thoughtfully. "Just when I think it's not possible to be any more in love with you than I am, you say something that makes me love you even more."

Dion said faintly: "*Love*?"

"Are you done with your breakfast, cherry?" Padraig took the fork from her nerveless fingers and put it across her unfinished meal. "Wonderful. I've been wanting to do this for weeks now."

If Dion hadn't been frozen in her seat, she could probably have avoided the kiss. It wasn't a cheeky thing like the one he had given Dion before she left him in Harlech, or the smothering thing that had happened in Bithywis: it came softly and gently, almost inevitably. Padraig pulled her to the edge of her seat, one hand at the small of her back and the other cupping her cheek, and Dion felt her heart start again with a shock. When he let her go, polished wood screeched against polished wood as she stood abruptly, knocking her chair back across the floor.

"Cherry," said Padraig, his hands out to his sides as if calming a skittish horse. "Now cherry, don't–"

Dion turned and whipped out of the room, hear heart pounding in her ears. She was halfway up the stairs before she realised that the common-room wasn't the most private place in which to retreat; but much to her relief, Barric was the only one there. He saw her face and was on his feet in a moment. "What is it?"

Dion turned her face away, but she could no more lie to Barric now than she could when she was a child. "It's nothing– I, um– Padraig kissed me."

Barric's dagger snicked back into its sheath with an ominously loud snap. "I'll go have a word with the Unseelie scab."

"No!" said Dion quickly, snatching at his arm. And if she was honest with herself, it wasn't really the kiss that had overthrown her so. What had overthrown her were the words that had come before. Her face was still hot and red, but she looked up at Barric properly anyway. He gazed down at her in surprise, and the smallest twitch of a smile came and went on his face.

"Did you run away?"

"Not really," Dion said. "Oh, I suppose so. I don't know what to do when he– oh, and what's the use, Barric? I'll be dead soon. What will happen to Padraig then?"

"Padraig can look after himself," said Barric. "He makes his own decisions– and he seems very determined about this one."

"Yes," said Dion feelingly. "*Very* determined."

"Is he making a nuisance of himself?"

"No!"

Again, Barric's scar pulled upward in a brief smile. "Then there's nothing to fuss about."

"No," said Dion again, more doubtfully. "Oh, bother. I have to go back." She heard a deep rumble and realised with some surprise that Barric was laughing. She didn't remember him laughing before. "It's all very funny now," she said, unable to stop the smile that sprang into being. "But just wait until you're in love and you don't know what to do about it."

The smile faded from Barric's lips, though his eyes still seemed to smile. "That won't be a problem," he said. "Go and talk to your Unseelie Fae. I have blades to clean."

"You always have blades to clean," said Dion; but she hugged him and left him to his knives anyway. Once outside the door, she took a deep breath and made herself walk back downstairs, anticipation and anxiety fluttering in her stomach. She almost abandoned her purpose with her fingers on the doorknob itself; but while she hesitated, Padraig's voice said softly from the other side of the boards: "I can hear you dithering, cherry. Am I to come out and fetch you?"

Dion froze; then, with an uncharacteristic burst of bravery, opened the door and slipped back in. Padraig was close enough both to her and the door that when he reached around her to close it, it left him with his arms around her. That, Dion was very well aware, was exactly how he wanted it, because he was smiling at her with a provocative amusement in his eyes.

"I'm sorry I ran away," she said, flushing under the constancy of that gaze. "I didn't mean– it's just that you keep taking me by surprise."

"Such a flatterer as you are, cherry! Are my kisses so dreadful?"

"No!' said Dion. "I v-very much enjoy them!"

"Oh, in that case–" Padraig took a swift step closer, cupping his hands around her face, and pressed a soft, warm kiss on her lips.

Dion didn't realise that tears had begun to glide down her cheeks until Padraig pulled back, smoothing them away with his thumbs. "Well now, what's there to cry about?" he demanded.

"Nothing," said Dion, wiping her cheeks on her sleeve. "You don't– I'm going to *die*, Padraig."

"Well, if it comes to that, so am I," said Padraig, and kissed her again.

"It's not the same! And there's so little time left: the sooner I die, the better for Llassar and the rest of the world."

"And can you," murmured Padraig, kissing first her jaw, then her cheekbone, then her lips: "Can you think of a better way of spending your last weeks than to love and be loved? To what better use could those weeks be put, cherry? Would you worry them away?"

Dion looked into his bright, lively eyes, and for the first time in many years felt very sure of one thing. She said: "No. I can't think of a better way to spend them."

Then, because Padraig's eyes were glowing down at her with an almost unbearable joy, she pulled his head back down and, for the first time, kissed him first.

"CARMINE, I THOUGHT YOU WANTED A BATH."

"I've had my bath," said Carmine, stretching out luxuriously on one of the window-seats. His hair was still damp and artfully disarrayed, and Dion noticed in some amusement that his shirt was only half-laced.

Kako wrinkled her nose. "Then what's that awful smell?"

"That, my Lady Dragon, is essence of violet," Carmine said, entirely unembarrassed. "Fancy loves it, don't you, Fancy?"

"Don't pull me into this," said Fancy.

"Try sleeping in the same room as that muck," said Padraig, absorbed in wrapping Dion's curls around his fingers. They had taken over the other window-seat, Dion leaning back into Padraig's arms and watching the room through half-closed eyes. Padraig was as thoroughly relaxed as Carmine; and Dion, who had at first been embarrassed and stiff when he pulled her close in front of the entire room, had found herself growing steadily more comfortable. "It creeps in at your nostrils and clings like sticky-briar."

"There's a beautiful thought," said Carmine lazily. "My Lady Dragon, you can't sit on my lap: Fancy wouldn't like it and she might hit me."

"Shove over, then," said Kako, her eyes on the street. Dion, watching them both with some amusement, thought that Kako must have quite a few siblings. "I don't want to worry anyone, but I think that shard we've been following since yesterday started following *us* this morning."

Dion sat straight up, her hand going instinctively to her shard. Kako was right: her shard was already hot to the touch. It probably had been for some time while she was distracted– at first by the simple pleasure of a good bath and then by Padraig downstairs. She would have felt guiltier about that if Kako's shard didn't affect her own enough to make the warmth seem normal by now.

"We've got to stop carrying the shards separately," she said. "It's making it too hard to tell when another one's getting nearer."

"I second that," said Kako. "Also, it might be a good idea to think about what we're going to do if the Fae start using humans to track us with shards, because I think they already *have*. Started, that is. Look."

Dion swivelled in dismay, her eyes darting to follow Kako's. Between two alehouses further along, there was a definite stirring in the already busy street.

"Up!" snarled Barric, his own eyes also on the disturbance.

Dion caught a brief glimpse of a young man looking down at something in his clasped hands, walking towards their inn at a swift pace. Behind him, glittering bright, was a company of well-armoured Fae. She was bundled away by Barric the next minute, hustled across the room to the windows on the other side. "Out."

"It won't do any good," she protested, trying to fend off Barric on one side and Padraig on the other. "They'll just follow us."

"True enough, but we don't choose to fight in close quarters," said Padraig. "Cherry, I love you dearly, but I'll not have you kicking me!"

"We can choose our ground outside," said Barric.

"We wouldn't make it further than the next street," said Dion, still resisting but unable to prevent herself being shoved out the window. At the same time, Kako said: "What, the streets? How is that better? It might be more open, but if we're brawling on the streets it will only be a matter of time before we're bothered by more Fae."

Padraig and Barric looked at each other. Barric gave a short, half nod. "All right," said Padraig. "Close quarters it is. But you stay outside, cherry. We'll barely have enough room for the three of us as it is."

"The three of us, who?" demanded Carmine. He sounded distinctly alarmed.

"You, me, the big man," said Padraig, with a sharp look at him.

"*I'm* not fighting!" said Carmine frankly. "Look at Barric's face! I'm not running that risk!"

Kako spluttered with laughter and launched herself from the window, wings fluttering into being and scales rippling over her body in the change. Rafiq followed close behind as Fancy said calmly: "He can't fight to save his life."

"Literally."

"Yes, literally," Fancy agreed. She withdrew her two long knives from the back of her jerkin, as slender and deadly as she herself. She smiled tranquilly at Padraig and Barric and added:

"Carmine, climb out the window with Dion. In quarters this close, if I cut you it will almost be an accident."

"This is why people aren't sure you love me," said Carmine; but he joined Dion outside on the roof.

"You'd better give me the shards, too," said Fancy to Dion. "I don't know how accurately that human is following us, but I'd rather they thought we're all in the room."

Barric set himself by the main door, Padraig by the connecting door that led down to the servants' quarters, and Fancy took her stance in the centre of the room, her back just slightly to Carmine and Dion. Dion watched her sadly, envious of her strong, graceful stance.

"This ought to be good," said Carmine, hanging blithely from the window frame. To Dion's astonishment, he didn't seem at all concerned about those of the group who were in the room.

"Why so glum, Princess?"

Dion stared at him. "Aren't you afraid for her?"

"For Fancy? Have you *seen* her fight?"

"Well, yes," admitted Dion. She knew exactly how well both Padraig and Barric fought, and she was still sick from terror that they would die this time. "But–"

"No buts," said Carmine. "That's the way to madness. Now I *could* be in there fighting, but I'd only be in Fancy's way and that would annoy her. Out here I can worry, but I find it more profitable to take in the beauty of her swordplay. And so much easier on the heart, too!"

"I suppose," said Dion. Still, Carmine's eyes honed in on Fancy as soon as the sound of assault began on the first door. Her own eyes went immediately to Padraig, and then to Barric; sick, anxious, and not entirely certain which way to look.

Barric's door was breached first. Dion jumped and made a small sound despite herself, but Barric only spun more lightly on his toes than anyone his size should have been able to move, sending the first Fae on through to Fancy. Fancy's blades crossed in a swift, decisive moment, and a Fae head went rolling.

"Beautiful!" said Carmine appreciatively, but Dion saw crimson magic licking around the fingers that had clenched involuntarily. Outside, Kako and Rafiq wheeled against the sky, diving lightning-fast through the houses to snatch the guarding Fae from the streets one by one; silent and deadly. Dion didn't see where they took the Fae, but this time there were no bloody heads or dismembered corpses dropping from the sky. The next time she looked down at the street it was empty of Fae.

The sound of splintering wood brought her attention back to the common-room: Padraig's door had split. He ducked, avoiding flying splinters of wood and the longsword that swiftly followed, and battered the longsword into the wreckage of the door with his hammer. Dion heard the furious sound of Fae swearing as the Fae on the other side of the half-broken door tried to wrench his longsword from the ruins.

"That'll teach you to bring a longsword to an indoor fight," Padraig advised the Fae, through the splintered door. Dion, her gaze winging to Barric, saw that he hadn't even drawn his massive greatsword: he was fighting hand to hand with a long knife and whichever of his throwing knives first came to hand. When neither of those was viable, he was punching the unhelmeted Fae. His knuckles were battered and slightly bloody, but Dion couldn't tell if the blood was his, or that of the Fae he had hit.

The fighting was at first reasonably orderly: the doors meant that the Fae could only attack one by one, and both Barric and Padraig disposed of those tidy attacks swiftly. Then, as the Fae began to apply their magical talents to breaking into the room, portions of the walls began to disappear and Fancy began to work in good earnest, dancing back and forth between Barric and Padraig.

"I don't want to watch this," said Dion, in sudden decision. "Let's go find the shard. Where do you think they've got it?"

"Downstairs, I suspect," said Carmine. He hissed between his teeth as a Fae dagger came far too close to Fancy's left eye, his fingers white about the windowsill. "If you've got a mind to find it, I'll come with you."

"All right," Dion said. The common-room was rapidly descending into a tight, mad, dangerous melee; and each time she saw Fancy slip a little in the blood that was slicked below her soft boots, she wondered if this was the moment she would throw up.

"After you, Princess," said Carmine. He offered Dion one arm and carefully lowered her until she could drop to the ground, then followed swiftly.

They re-entered the inn by the kitchen door. It was empty and in a state of considerable disorder, as though the maid and cook had been chased out in something of a hurry. As they approached the swinging door to the taproom, Dion caught at Carmine's sleeve and whispered: "It's in there."

Even without her own shard to pinpoint the other, she could sense the unmistakeably strong Fae magic that emanated from the taproom.

Carmine was already nodding. "I know," he said. She saw a brief flash of uncertainty in his eyes, but it was gone almost immediately. He winked at her and threw open the swinging door to the taproom. There were two Fae in the room; one of them sitting at his ease with the shard resting on his knee, and the other squarely between his companion and the door. There was no sign of the human who had led them, and Dion was caught between hope that they had merely sent him on his way and dread that his corpse was lying somewhere around the inn.

"Just imagine!" said the Fae who was standing. "The banished princess of Llassar, here in Shinpo!"

"I'm flattered, but should you invest in a pair of glasses?" said Carmine. "I may be beautiful, but I'm not quite feminine."

The seated Fae gave them both a look of disgust. "You fool. Have you tired of living?"

"That's a question you should be asking your friends upstairs, I think," said Carmine. He was making small, flicking motions behind his back at Dion, his fingers dripping with scarlet magic. Instead of heeding them, Dion took her place beside him.

The seated Fae smiled at her, his beautiful face cold and smooth. "You shouldn't have wandered from home, daughter of Ywain. Have you heard the reports of your sister? The skirmishes are not going well for her, but there are consolations. They're calling her Aerwn ferch Pobl, daughter of the people. Even if events turn as you wish, she's stolen your throne."

"It never was mine," said Dion. "And you're the fool if you think that matters. Give us the shard."

"I think not," said the Fae who was standing. There was a steely slither, and his gold-tinted Fae blades were there in each hand, light and comfortable. He didn't give either Dion or Carmine a chance to react; he simply lunged, point high and deadly. Dion threw up her hand, manipulating the air currents to tilt it higher still, and it hissed past her ear. The other blade slicked back toward them, but it met Carmine instead of Dion. Dion, stumbling back from a decided shove from Carmine's crimson magic, saw it slice along his abdomen, severing shirt and skin alike, and heard the groan he gave. It made her realise that the shuffle of the Fae's feet, the sweep of his blade, and Carmine's panting breath were the only sounds she had heard since the Fae had first struck. The clanks and thumps from upstairs had ceased entirely. Dion threw a sharp edge of magic, turning aside the Fae's blade as he brought it back on Carmine, and ducked beneath the attack he directed at her. The Fae had on magic-repellent armour, which made her feel queasy; but when it occurred to her that neither of his swords were protected, she threw them toward the ceiling.

The standing Fae was thrown to the ceiling with his swords

and pinned there by their hilts. He spat a series of poisonous spells at Dion, who deflected them with a spinning web of magic that caught each one and flicked it away safely.

The other Fae stood at last, gracefully, his beautiful hands spread from his sides. He had no armour on at all, and no weapons except a small dagger. Dion experienced a sinking feeling that suggested this Fae only bare of weapons because he didn't need them.

Carmine seemed to have the same idea. He murmured: "Offence or defence?"

"Defence," said Dion, and threw up a shield just in time. The Fae's magic struck it with shattering force, throwing her backwards, and Carmine caught her around the waist.

"We'll dance another time, shall we?" he said. And then: "Oh, just in time! Reinforcements!"

Barric was looming, huge and deadly, behind the Fae. He must have come down the stairs. Dion saw the Fae smiling just before he whirled, a deadly shaft of magic singing from his fingers at Barric, and screamed. There was an instant between her understanding and the moment she felt the burn of death magic searing her fingertips, unasked and unexpected. A shard of obsidian sliced through the Fae from navel to neck, tearing his torso in half. He made a rather peculiar noise, and dropped to his knees, in a splattering of blood and gore.

"Oh, beautifully done!" said Carmine, with relish. "Whoops, *down*, Princess!"

Dion was tackled to the ground, the hair on the back of her head prickling as a sharp-edged spell ripped past. Instinctively recoiling from the body of the Fae she had killed, she saw Barric tearing the other from the ceiling by the neck. There was a sickening kind of snap that seemed to stick in her mind, and then Padraig was lifting her to her feet.

"Cherry? Cherry, are you well?"

Dion looked into his concerned eyes and then down at her

hands. It felt like they should be burned, but they were only shaking. "Yes. Um. I killed him."

"Beautiful job, too," said Fancy, observing the dead Fae with an impartial eye. "A bit messy, but effective. Carmine, you'll have to take your shirt off."

"Darling, you had only to ask," said Carmine immediately. He was bleeding a little, but not seriously. To Dion, he said: "You're a trifle pale, Princess."

"S-so are you," said Dion, fighting with a sob that wanted to come out. "Thanks for saving my life."

"Let's just say I was repaying the favour," Carmine said, winking at her. "For all the good it did me– at this rate, I'll be the only one without a kill to my name."

"You can have mine," said Dion, shuddering. "I don't want it."

"LIVELY THINGS, THESE SHARDS," said Carmine. He had put on another shirt, but as usual it wasn't properly laced and he was looking very heroic and pale. "Following us around wherever we go."

"It's all rather nice, isn't it?" said Fancy. "We could have stayed where we were and the shards would have come to *us*. A bit of inconvenience, a few scratches–"

"Scratches!" said Carmine, almost beside himself. "My darling cactus, I refuse to have my life-threatening wound dismissed as a scratch!"

"Oh, but it makes you look so dashing!" Fancy said, grinning.

"Only if he goes around shirtless all the time," Dion said dispassionately.

"He does," said Fancy and Padraig at the same time.

"Time to go," said Kako, popping her head in around the door. "Fae corps are closing in fast from the next town."

"Where next?" said Padraig, when they were all on the street. Everyone seemed to take it for granted that Dion and Kako were leading; and they had each started out in the same direction without so much as a shared glance. "We shouldn't be out on the streets, think on."

"There's another shard toward the north-east," said Dion, and Kako silently assented. "In Illisr. But if the Fae have started using human guides–"

"We're going to have to be more careful."

Dion, exchanging a glance with Kako, said: "What about the other one?"

Barric frowned. "What other one?"

"We can sense another shard: Montalier, I think," said Kako. "It's stronger than the other ones. Don't you think, Dion?"

"It's stronger," agreed Dion. "Montalier or Illisr first?"

"Illisr," said Kako and Rafiq together.

"Why Illisr?"

"It's quicker," said Rafiq. "Not if you travel by land, but on the wing it's quicker to go from here to Illisr and then on to Montalier."

"What I want to know," said Kako; "Is why everything is so wonderfully convenient? My shard didn't start being attracted to other shards until about five weeks ago, which coincided *marvellously* with the attack on the castle. I suppose what I'm really wondering is, is this another Fae trick? If they can use the shards to find us by using humans to track us, could it be that they're the ones who made the shards so suddenly easy to find? I find it highly suspicious that the shards only became drawn to each other when we began to search for them."

"So do I," said Fancy, but Padraig said: "It wasn't the Fae. The shards began to be attracted to each other as soon as Dion came of age, isn't that right, cherry? Your seventeenth birthday fell five weeks ago just before I met you in Bithywis."

"Well, someone slotted you into the prophecy very nicely!" said Kako, unerringly leading the way through a thin gap between someone's house and an orchard wall. It opened onto a stretch of flat, soggy ground that was more than slightly squishy. "Just like a handy little cog in a big, complicated machine."

Fancy looked slightly horrified, but Dion laughed. "It is a bit like that."

"Come now, cherry," said Padraig, swinging her hand. "Surely not a cog! The heart-mechanism, think on!"

"Yes, but that doesn't work so well as an analogy," Kako pointed out. "Cogs can be slipped in and out. The heart-mechanism doesn't get slotted in: it's worked on *in* the machine and can't be removed."

"Then I stand by my remarks," said Padraig loftily.

"As far as I know, I could be removable," Dion said. "Suppose I'd died before my seventeenth birthday? Aerwen is Ywain's daughter, too: wouldn't the prophecy just slot her in instead of me?"

"The real question is, why *didn't* you die before your seventeenth birthday?" said Fancy unexpectedly. "If I were the Fae, I wouldn't want a potential little Ywain's daughter running around."

"Do you know," said Dion slowly; "I think they didn't. But I think they thought Aerwn was Ywain's daughter. She was the one always pushing and rebelling, and she was the one they always went after. They had us thinking she was mentally unstable for years!" She stopped at the thought, a fresh poniard of horror and self-blame lancing her heart. How much had Aerwn suffered not just because of Dion's inability to believe her, but because of Dion's self?

Padraig's blue eyes glanced at her. "Aerwn *is* mentally unstable," he said, with an easy grin. "She turned out remarkably well for it."

"What's done is done," said Barric: the first he had spoken in some time. Dion wondered anxiously if he had been made to feel uncomfortable by the comparison of herself to a cog, considering his part in the prophecy and her involvement in it; and had another twinge of self-blame. "You didn't die and the prophecy will be fulfilled. There's no use trying to change the course of history."

"Oh, *that's* rich!" said Carmine, his eyes dancing. "A Guardian saying that there's no use trying to change history!"

Barric gave him a look. "We'd best be taking to the sky. Time is not our friend."

"Oh, and that reminds me," said Kako. She looked perfectly innocent, but both Barric and Carmine looked at her narrowly.

"What reminds you?" asked Carmine, with deep foreboding.

"What Barric said about not being friends," explained Kako. "Well, neither is Illisr. Not to Rafiq and me, anyway. I slightly killed one of their princes while I was trying to get Rafiq out of his clutches, so Illisr isn't the best place for him to be. Once we're within sniff of the border patrols we'll have to change back to our human forms. It'll take longer to get there, but at least you won't find yourselves captured because of us."

Barric nodded. "Is there anything else we should know about Illisr?"

"Apart from it being a nasty place to stay and peopled by a race only just less inclined to think themselves superior to everyone else than the Fae? No."

"And are there any other countries that want to capture or kill you on sight?"

"Wait, I want to know how you can slightly kill a prince," protested Fancy.

"No," said Kako sunnily. "Everyone else adores us. Well, they adore me: they *love* Rafiq. That's what happens when you're ridiculously good looking and the only exotic man in a three-country span."

To Dion's huge delight, this matter-of-fact statement sent blush winging across Rafiq's face. It was difficult to see against the darkness of his skin, but she saw it rising in his neck and in the glow of his face, and when he saw her watching he immediately began to change to his dragon form.

Kako only laughed. "That's the quickest way I know to make him change," she said.

"Do we have to compliment you, or will you change by yourself?" asked Carmine.

"Oh no," said Kako, with a rather dragonish grin. "You only have to make me angry."

Barric's scar pulled sidewise in a brief smile. "Are there any other complications we should know about?"

"We should be fine, so long as we stay out of the capital," said Kako, beginning to ripple into her dragon form in an iridescence of scales. "But you know what they say about the Unprepared being the Fools of the Court of Reason."

They arrived close by the Illisrian border at evening two days later, stopping only to allow Rafiq and Kako to change into their human forms. Much to Dion's surprise, the shard she and Kako had sensed while in Shinpo had not moved while they flew from southern Shinpo to the Illisrian border. She was quite sure of it, because Kako and Barric had both given her the shards they were carrying, and it was now a very easy matter to sense where the other shards were. The fact that she couldn't sense the seventh shard at all had begun to worry her a little; but more immediately worrying was the lack of movement of the fifth shard.

"Maybe no one knows it's there," she said hopefully. "Maybe no one is looking after it at all."

Barric didn't answer, but his thumb brushed the pommel of his long dagger. Dion recognised the gesture immediately: Barric was expecting trouble.

"I'd lay you odds it's a trap," said Padraig, "but I'd not wish to steal from you, cherry."

"Then what should we do? If it's a trap–"

"–then we spring it," Padraig said, a light of enjoyment in his sapphire eyes. "Have you ever seen a furry Long-tail spring a trap, cherry?"

"No," said Dion, whose quarters had always been mercifully free of the rat-like pests.

"He always makes sure that something else is in the trap when he springs it. And then he takes the bait and leaves the other poor, unfortunate animal in the trap while he skips merrily on his way."

"Us being the Long-tail in this scenario?" said Kako. She didn't sound quite convinced.

"Even so," nodded Padraig.

Still, when they had found the place that housed the Illisrian shard, it didn't *look* like a trap. Dion was already feeling anxious: all of the shards they had collected to date were bundled in her pack, wrapped so that they didn't rattle against each other, and she was feeling distinctly noticeable. It didn't help that Barric and Padraig were both several streets away with Kako and Rafiq– or that she had insisted upon it herself. Barric had agreed that Padraig and she should be separated in expectation of a trap, but he hadn't been happy to leave her to the sole guardianship of Fancy and Carmine.

The place was a shop; old and dusty-windowed. Dion was much relieved to see that the shop-keeper was human. He welcomed them in, his eyes darting curiously from face to face as if he wasn't quite sure what to make of their exotically pale skin. He seemed both convinced and interested when they told him they were simply travelling from Llassar to Illisr for the Festival of Lanterns; but though he was unsuspicious, he was more than slightly inconvenient. He followed them about the store, chattering almost without pausing for breath, and it was only when Carmine engaged him in conversation with a small, encouraging flick of the fingers at Dion, that she was able to search the store without the shop-keeper's sharp eyes upon her.

She knew immediately where the shard was: the difficulty was in keeping her eyes from straying in that direction while the shopkeeper still watched them so curiously. When she was free of his gaze, Dion went straight to it. Someone had mounted it on a piece of polished wood with a tiny plaque that declared it to be 'the last piece of Dhoni Kumba's sword'; which was rather clever, Dion thought. It was the hilt-piece, and rather bigger than she'd expected. She didn't touch it immediately, because there was a sly, almost unnoticeable spell on it, and she wanted to know what it was before she activated it by picking up the shard.

"You'd best hurry," said Fancy, in a low voice. "His little eyes are darting all over the shop, trying to see you. I don't know if he's part of all this or if he just thinks we're likely to steal from him, but even Carmine won't be able to keep him there much longer."

"It *is* a trap," said Dion. "But I think I can spring it safely."

Fancy's hands instinctively rose to her shoulders in search of her knife hilts. "Where are the Fae?"

"Not here. I think they're keeping their distance so they don't frighten us away."

"That's a bit stupid of them," said Fancy.

"Not really," Dion said slowly. "I can't actually remove the spell, and as soon as I tinker with it, the Fae will know. After I start, we'll only a have a few minutes at the most before they get here."

"All right," said Fancy. "What do you need us to do?"

"Grab the shop keeper and sit on him," said Dion. "I'm going to pin the spell on him instead."

"With pleasure!" Fancy said, and hurried back to the other side of the shop. Dion heard a brief scuffle, then the sound of the sign in the front door being flipped.

Carmine's voice called: "Would you care for delivery, madam?"

"Yes, please," returned Dion, grinning. She didn't dare to move the shard until the spell was activated, and she preferred not to activate it herself. Fancy and Carmine made their way between displays, cheerfully carrying the terrified shop-keeper between them, and deposited him at her feet. His popping eyes stared wildly up at her, and Dion said kindly: "Don't worry. I'm only going to get you to pick up this curio. That's all right, isn't it?"

The shopkeeper flailed desperately, scrabbling against the floor until Fancy, rolling her eyes, actually did sit on him.

"I take it you know what the spell does," said Carmine, his eyes very narrow. "And I'm guessing that it's not a particularly nice one. Well now, you've got two choices, my talkative little friend. Either you pick up the curio, or I cut off your hand. Which would you prefer?"

The shop-keeper said something muffled into the carpet.

"My darling, perhaps you could allow the poor fellow to take his face out of the carpet."

"All right," said Fancy. "But if he tries to bite me again, I'll knock all of his teeth out. Got it?"

The shop-keeper made another muffled noise, which seemed to satisfy Fancy, because she allowed him to rise.

"We'll have to be quick," Dion warned. "The Fae will know as soon as I trip the spell." She knew it was a mistake as soon as she said it: the shopkeeper's eyes flashed, and he snatched the shard up before she could stop him. Dion yelped, her hands reacting almost before her mind did. Her right hand flicked a touch of magic that hove the shard free from its mount while her left hand pinched outward, expanding a domed barrier over the shop-keeper. She leapt away from the dome almost the next moment, fearful of being touched by the spell that was still seeping through her barrier.

"*What* was that?" demanded Carmine, his eyes even more narrow than before. Within Dion's domed barrier, the shop-keeper had frozen, his hand still on the mounting that had held the shard. The shard itself had caught in mid-air just beyond

Dion's barrier. No, not exactly stopped; slowed. It still moved, but barely.

"Get back!" Dion said sharply. "My barrier isn't filtered narrowly enough to keep it all in."

"What is it?"

"There was a targeted time spell on the shard," said Dion, cautiously circling closer to the shard while Fancy went to check their way out.

"How do we get the shard if it's frozen?"

"It's not exactly frozen," Dion said, biting her lip. "It's just moving through time more slowly than we are. I think. We'll have to wait for it to come out of the influence of the spell before we can touch it."

"How long will that take?" called Fancy, from the front door.

"I don't know."

Carmine's brows rose. "That's unfortunate. One of us will have to wait here."

"We'll all–"

"No, we won't," said Fancy. "And you can't argue when you made Padraig stay outside for the same reason. Carmine and I will stay until the shard leaves the spell. You join Barric and the others."

"I'll send one of the dragons back," said Dion tightly.

"Best hurry," Carmine said significantly. "I feel a storm brewing."

Dion knew what he meant as soon as she left the shop. There was a pushing sensation of built-up magic rolling in fast from the west: a significant amount of Fae were swiftly approaching. She broke into a run, the hairs standing up on the back of her neck. Barric caught her as she sprinted around the next street corner, his scarred face light with relief, and said: "Where are the others?"

"With the shard," Dion said. "It's coming, but they need more time."

"I can buy them time," said Barric.

Rafiq nodded. "As can I."

"Oh, no you don't!" Kako said at once. "They *know* you here. I'll go with Barric: you take Padraig and Dion. Don't change until it's safe."

"You'll go with Rafiq and Padraig," Barric said to Dion, but she heard the question in his voice.

She sighed. "Yes. But–"

"I'll make sure they're safe."

The street was dark and silent as they ran. Away from the town centre, Fae lanterns were fewer, and Dion knew it wouldn't be long before Rafiq was safe to change. She felt the vast blockage of Fae behind them at the edges of her mind: a dam waiting to burst. She shivered, afraid for the others and sick at running away.

"This greatly smacks of running away," said Padraig, as if he'd read her mind.

"I know," she said shortly. "But–"

Padraig's eyes met hers for a brief moment. "I know."

Rafiq segued from man to dragon the next instant, his shadow sweeping vast and dark against the passing walls. He stopped briefly to allow them to climb on, and then launched effortlessly into the air. If Rafiq's human walk was not quite so smooth as Kako's, his launch was far smoother than hers.

Padraig's voice said in Dion's ear: "Did anyone see us?"

"I don't think so," she said. Her eyes anxiously searched the Fae-lit streets below as they flew overhead. There! There was Barric, sweeping wide and strong with his greatsword. Fancy danced beside him, her blades cutting through Fae-light and Fae flesh alike, and Kako was behind, sending bright sparks of magic into the enemy that sought out the unarmoured Fae. Mingling with the Fae were Illisrian soldiers, their bows levelled at Kako. As Dion watched, Padraig clutched at her arm.

"There!"

Carmine burst from the shop below, a glint of Fae-light from the public lanterns betraying the presence of the shard in his left hand. Kako whirled and changed in an instant, Carmine clinging to her back and Fancy and Barric leaping to join him as she barrelled past them, charging the Fae.

"And we're off!" said Padraig gleefully.

They had already outstripped the scene below; but Dion, who craned her head to the very last moment, cried out. The Fae that Kako had charged were sending filaments of sticky magic after her: they clung to her wings and dragged her down.

Dion didn't hear a sound, but Rafiq must have caught a mental trace of distress from Kako, because he wheeled in the air without warning. Padraig yelled, and Dion felt him seize her waist convulsively as they both lurched in their seats. Rafiq made a stomach-churning dive, molten fire blasting a swathe through the Fae below, and Dion felt the heat of magic in her fingers. She slashed through the nearest filaments that pulled dangerously at Kako's wings, and saw Carmine's startled, understanding face as they bypassed the others in a singeing torrent of displaced air. When she looked back, he was doing the same thing. Kako, her huge wings beating in laboured strokes, began to rise again.

Something stung Dion's cheek. She blinked, swiping at a tickle of what turned out to be blood, and saw another arrow streak by Rafiq's massive head. Filaments of sticky magic followed, thick and fast, as both Fae and Illisrian soldiers turned their attention from Kako to Rafiq.

Padraig pounded Rafiq's back. "Go, go! She's free!"

Dion snatched away sticky Fae magic as she saw it attach to Rafiq's wings, but Rafiq's shoulder muscles still strained with the effort of rising. Dealing with the magic left her no attention spare to ward off the arrows, and she heard Rafiq's roar as two of the arrows pierced his left wing, dripping steaming blood on the rooftops below. Kako shot past them at speed, both Carmine and Barric leaning out perilously to slash through the remaining magic that weighed on Rafiq, and Dion felt a sudden lurch as they were free to rise. It was a ragged ascent: Rafiq's left wing was losing not only blood but air.

Dion heard Kako's voice say grimly in her mind: *Rafiq, stop and change.*

A few more miles, said Rafiq's voice, just as grimly.

"We can't stop yet!" said Padraig. "There's too many Fae, sure!"

"Arrows!" yelled Fancy.

Dion spun a defensive spell from her fingers, but even as it arched beneath the dragons to join with Barric's defence, Padraig gasped and lost his grip on her waist. She looked around at the empty space behind her in wild confusion, and heard the distant sound of something hitting the roof-tops below. Padraig, his body as limp as a rag-doll, slid down one of the roofs and dropped heavily into the darkness of the street.

She heard Carmine shout, "Man overboard!" but she was already stretching down, reaching further than she had ever reached, to find the time-slowing spell that had begun it all. She broke away the barrier she had made around it, feeding a furious chunk of her own magic into it; and it grew immediately and vastly, encapsulating both the Fae and Illisrian soldiers in a moment.

"Up!" shouted Barric, an edge of fear in his voice, and both dragons shot high into the night, away from the heaviness of slowed time.

"We have to go back for Padraig!" screamed Dion. She was already scrambling free of Rafiq's neck, clumsy in her haste, when he landed heavily on another of the rooftops. Kako came to a more elegant stop in a swirl of heated air, depositing her passengers without notice as she resumed her human form.

"Very pretty," she said to Dion. "But did you catch Padraig in there, too?"

"Maybe," Dion said, holding back hot tears. She couldn't afford to be sick or tearful right now. "I think so. We're on the right street, but I don't know how far back he fell. And I don't know where the arrow—"

"Shoulder," said Fancy briskly. "High up. He'll be fine."

"He wasn't moving," Dion said. She took the hand that Barric offered her, and was lowered gently from the roof to a balcony below.

Fancy, dropping down beside her, said lightly, "Must have hit his head;" which would have been comforting had not Dion seen the slight grimace that pulled across Fancy's lips.

Dion was the first one on the street, and she didn't wait for the others. It was darker here, away from the high street, and she stopped briefly at each alley and road that opened onto her own with the fretful fear that she would miss seeing Padraig.

The others were spread out behind and beside her, following her lead, and Carmine's voice floated up to her. "What was it someone was saying about being unprepared?"

"Shut up, Carmine," suggested Kako's voice, in a friendly fashion.

"Something about being fools," continued Carmine. "And a court of reason. One hardly cares to make snap judgements, but—"

"You can't say we were unprepared," said Dion miserably, taking a few steps down another street. There was no sign of Padraig here, either, and she could feel the time-slowing spell beginning to falter up ahead. The Fae hadn't designed it to be quite so large. "We had a plan."

"Big man, your protective spells aren't particularly protective," said Carmine, evidently determined upon mischief. "All in all, I can't help feeling that you leave something to be desired as a Guardian. Is that *cabbage*? Fancy, I've been made to stand in liquid *cabbage*, and if you roll your eyes at me—"

Barric ignored it, but Dion flashed, "Barric couldn't help it! It was my spell that wasn't quick enough to stop the arrows."

"That's no excuse," Carmine said firmly. "He's the Guardian, and–"

There was the wet, slapping sound of old vegetables hitting something soft.

"Ow!" said Carmine, outraged. "Was that you, Fancy?"

"No," said Dion, flushing hot in the darkness but still annoyed enough to make her voice clipped. "It was m-me!"

"Fancy," Carmine said, in a pained voice. "Remind me not to insult Guardians around the tender young waifs they protect."

"I could say something about fools," said Fancy's voice dryly. "But–"

"Fancy, I won't have my mockingly quoted words quoted mockingly at me."

"What are you going to do about–"

"There," said Barric, speaking at last. Dion saw a ripple of light glowing against the cobbles: it flowed across the stones and gently lit a supine form that was caught in free-fall a bare yard above the street. Even Carmine was silenced for a moment.

Then he said: "Yes, beautifully done; but how do we get him *out?*"

"The spell is weakening," said Barric. "We've only to wait. Dion, can you–"

"Yes," said Dion, who had already seen Barric's magic carefully insinuating itself between the time-spell and the cobbles: a cushion with which to catch Padraig when he eventually fell. She coated a patch of the spell closest to Padraig with a veneer of her own magic, her eyes anxiously upon the arrow that was protruding from his shoulder both at his chest and his back. And as her magic ate away at the time-spell, Dion clasped one hand in the other, her fingers white and just barely shaking.

When Padraig dropped into Barric's netted magic, heavy and limp, he was whisked away from the rest of the spell immediately.

"Best to get that out right away," opined Fancy, looking at the arrow with something of a professional eye. Barric nodded, snapping off head and fletch effortlessly, and stood aside to let Fancy draw out the shaft.

"We'll have to heal him as we fly," Dion said. The time-spell was fading rapidly now, and she was almost as anxious to be in the air as she was for Padraig. Rafiq grew darkly in the shadows of the over-arching houses, wedging himself tightly between the surrounding houses, and crouched low to allow Dion to climb on his back. She settled herself and reached out as Barric half-lifted, half-levitated Padraig up in front of her, and when she threw an anxious look at Rafiq's left wing, prepared for a rough launch, she discovered that it was whole. Instead of a large hole, there was a large scar.

"Neat trick, isn't it?" said Kako, leaping lightly back onto the balcony. "That's another thing I've got theories about, but what with the shards and everything, I haven't had time to explore it. Come on, you two. We're launching from the roof, *if* you don't mind. I'm not as strong as Rafiq."

Carmine and Fancy followed her effortlessly as Barric wedged himself behind Dion, his huge arms around both her and Padraig. Dion, her own arms wrapped so tightly around Padraig that they ached, lurched back into Barric's chest as Rafiq began a crawling climb straight up one of the houses. When his wings were free, he sprang up and away from the wall, sending plaster and brick-dust showering into the cobbles below. Barric's arms tightened briefly, but when Rafiq's flight evened out, one of his hands spread wide across Padraig's shoulder, covering bloody cloth and flesh alike.

Dion, her eyes still hot with tears, held Padraig tightly and watched as Barric's magic flowed into his chest. It trickled out bit by bit, carefully and slowly, as Illisr passed swiftly beneath them in indistinguishable darkness.

When at last the trickle of magic cease, Dion tilted her head back to look nervously at Barric. "Is– is he–"

"He'll live," said Barric. "For now. There's a little bleeding inside that I haven't been able to stop, but I'll look at it again when he's rested."

It wasn't until long after the ache in Dion's arms dulled to numbness that a twin gleam of sapphire in the moonlight caught her attention. Padraig's eyes had opened a slit.

"You're a pleasant sight to wake up to," he murmured. "Cherry, did you rescue me again? Sure, I'm beginning to feel that I might be a damsel in distress!"

Dion dropped her head into his healthy shoulder, allowing the glad tears to catch warmly in his collar. "You are," she said; and in her relief, with a burr in her voice that might have been either a laugh or a sob, she added: "It's a good thing you're so pretty."

Padraig spluttered a laugh to the moon, and as the lights of the town behind them faded to a single speck of light, Fancy's voice, carrying clearly, said: "Don't try to cuddle me, Carmine; you smell like cabbage."

GETTING into Montalier unseen was difficult: Montalier's army were clearly on high alert, and the borders were not only patrolled but properly guarded. Kako and Rafiq had to fly so high in an effort to avoid notice that their human passengers became dangerously cold and short of breath.

Getting into Montalier's capital city was even harder: the guards were on the lookout for Fae, both Seelie and Unseelie, and it took a swift bit of magic on Dion's part to bring Padraig through unnoticed. Barric, she saw, didn't have a similar problem. Apparently it wasn't just Dion who didn't recognised his magic as Fae.

But it wasn't until they had traced the shard through the city streets that the full difficulty of their situation burst upon them.

"Oh," said Kako. "That's really unfortunate."

"Unfortunate!" Dion said, dropping her pack in despair. "The shard is in the castle. How are we supposed to get into the castle?"

"You're a princess, cherry," said Padraig, who was still rather pale. "Be regal. Demand an audience."

"That won't work," said Dion, at the same time that Barric said simply: "No."

"Of course it will," Carmine said. He looked surprised. "They're not the sort to stand on ceremony."

"You didn't see the letter my father sent Montalier when they invited me for a month-long visit," Dion said gloomily. "Montalier has been the single biggest threat to the Fae invasion beside Avernse: I can't see the king giving up their shard to the Princess Heir of the first country that dealt with the Fae. Why would they trust me?"

"And it's no use looking at me," said Kako. "My mother and elder sister have met the family, but I've never been here before. I haven't even got a royal seal, if it comes to that."

"And once they know we're coming, we'll lose our edge of surprise, think on," said Padraig. "Dion's in the right. We should try to steal it."

"Hopefully without getting captured this time," added Kako. "There are a lot of enchantments around the castle."

"Dion and I will deal with those," said Barric. He didn't sound particularly worried; but then, he rarely did. Dion, who could also see the strength and the intricacy of the protective spells on the castle, *was* worried.

"Oh well," said Carmine. He seemed to be highly amused, though Dion wasn't quite sure why. "Why not, after all? It could be enjoyable to steal from Montalier."

"Don't enjoy yourself too much," said Fancy, and Dion thought she heard an undercurrent of sharpness to the woman's voice. What was that about?

"Fancy!" said Carmine, a bright glitter of delight in his eyes. "You do care!"

Fancy, her sensible face a little flushed, said: "Oh, just get on with the planning! Are we all to take part in this desperate venture?"

"The more the merrier, my darling; the more the merrier!"

"Yes," said Dion. "Well, we'll have to leave as soon as we've got it, won't we? The Fae in Illisr said the fight in Llassar wasn't going well, and we've already been too long about it all. We've still got another shard to find yet."

"We stick together this time," nodded Barric. "And if we're to surmount the castle defences, we'll need to take to the skies again."

It wouldn't have occurred to Dion that the wards around the castle would be any less stringent the higher they flew. Llassar— like Montalier, evidently—wasn't used to the idea of aerial assault, and she was shocked beyond measure to find that there were gaps in the ward that birds could easily fly through. For all Dion knew, that's what the gaps were for. But it was only the work of a few minutes to convince the wards that Kako and Rafiq *were* birds, albeit very large ones, and for the dragons to begin a silent descent toward the roof that was nearest to the shard.

"There's a window open," said Kako, when they were all safely on the roof.

"And a guard on the widow's walk above," Barric said softly. "Keep to the wall and keep your voices down."

"Yes, but there's a *window open*," argued Kako. "Well, half a window, anyway; but if that's not suspicious, I don't know what is."

"You sleep with the windows open," pointed out Rafiq. "And it *is* the small half."

"Yes, but I can turn into a dragon."

"Maybe the person who sleeps in there can turn into a dragon," said Carmine gaily. He had only grown merrier.

"It's not a bedroom," said Dion, who had been peering through the glass. "It's more of a gallery."

Fancy and Barric exchanged a glance, and Padraig said: "Suspicious, then. We're agreed. Who'll go in first?"

"I will," said Dion. "No; *listen* to me. None of the men will fit, and if I get caught, well, like Padraig says: I'm a princess."

"You might as well let her," said Carmine. Of all the group, he was easily the most light-hearted. Dion wondered what he knew that the rest of them didn't. "She'll come to no harm in there."

Barric thought about it while Padraig protested, and then said above Padraig's objections: "All right. In you go."

He lifted her carefully and helped her to slip through. Dion, feeling a lot less sure of herself than she pretended, looked back over her shoulder once. The sight of Barric's huge shadow against the stars calmed her, and she stole further into the darkened room, her feet light against the carpeted floor. Where the single shard rested above her heart there was a decided warmth, a physical manifestation of the magical reaction she had been feeling ever since they had begun to seek shards. She stepped lightly across the floor, her senses open for both magical and physical traps, and passed through the door into the next room almost without pausing. The shard was further in. She was so intent on her steps that she didn't feel the difference in the air of the second room—the way that the darkness folded around a warmth in one corner—until a male voice said: "There's nothing worth stealing in these rooms, you know."

Dion started violently, her breath choking in the back of her throat, and gasped the first question that came to mind. "Then why are you here?"

She heard the sound of fingers snapping and the room lit softly from a globe that hovered above her head. The shadowed warmth proved to be a rather pleasant-faced man with kind eyes and dark hair that was silvering over his temples.

He said: "Althea thought someone would be along today. She didn't want to frighten you, so here I am."

Dion found herself coughing a small laugh. "I'm always frightened," she said bleakly.

A smile spread over his face, making the same kind of lines by his eyes that Barric had. The twisting of fear in Dion's stomach released its stranglehold at the sight of them, and she let out a shaky breath that she'd been holding.

"I won't hurt you," he said. "But we do have to talk."

"Yes," Dion agreed. "You said there's nothing to steal in here, but you were waiting *here*. And you didn't give me a proper answer, either. You know I came to steal the shard and I know the shard is here. Who are you?"

He gazed at her thoughtfully. "I really feel like I should be the one asking that question."

"I'm Dion ferch Ywain," said Dion baldly. "I've committed treason against the Crown and my sister is at war with our own parents. Stealing the shard from Montalier didn't seem so bad after that."

"I suppose it wouldn't," agreed the man. He bowed just deeply enough to indicate equal acknowledging equal. "I'm Markon. I'm the king around here."

Dion's mouth dropped open slightly and she scrambled into something that was half-curtsey, half-bow. "Oh! I'm s-so sorry! But we *have* to have the shard, your majesty! We can't seal up the land without it!"

Markon's face seemed to lighten. "I see. In that case, it's probably best if you speak with my wife."

"The enchantress," said Dion, her throat a little dry. Her father had told her about the Avernsian enchantress– but then, he had told her a lot of things that weren't true.

"That's right. I'm afraid I can't offer much help myself: I'm not very well educated when it comes to magic."

"That's quite all right," Dion said, inanely polite. "I mean– is she awake?"

"I'd be surprised if she wasn't listening from the next room, actually," said Markon. He called out: "She's supposed to be resting more than usual, but I'm not quite sure she knows how. You can come in now, dear."

There was a dignified silence before the handle in the door behind him turned. A very pregnant young woman stepped briskly into the room, surprising Dion with her youthfulness. Dion glanced back at Markon in time to see the softer light that sprang to his eyes at the sight of the woman, and the deep delight of his smile. He looked as if he hadn't seen her all day– or perhaps all week. Althea gave him back a prim look with her dark blue eyes dancing.

"Isn't it lucky I was passing?" she said. She looked Dion up and down frankly, while Dion became very horribly aware of the Fae magic that curled tightly within Althea, then said unexpectedly: "It's all right. It's not mine. Well, it is, but I'm not Fae."

Dion looked again, fascinated. "How? It's– I mean, I can see it now, but *how*? How do you have Fae magic when you're human?"

"I killed a Fae king and ran away from Faery when I was eighteen." Althea stopped with a rather peculiar expression on her face, and pressed a hand to her side. When Markon stepped swiftly forward she smacked him in the stomach with the back of her hand. "Ow! Your daughter kicked me again."

"She's going to be just like her mother," said Markon amiably. Dion was amused to see that he seemed to be quite used to being hit.

Althea, unashamed, continued to gaze at Dion. "So you're Alawn ap Fane's daughter."

Dion grimaced minutely. "No. I'm Ywain's daughter."

Althea's eyes rested on her thoughtfully. "That's understandable, I suppose. I tried to arrange to visit you when I found out how much of Ywain's magical line had passed on to you. Your father wasn't very accommodating."

"No, he isn't," said Dion slowly, remembering a night—almost faded to ancient nightmare now—when she had listened the same voice she had heard and loved for years declaring her guilt and judgement.

"It's unfortunate," Althea said. There was a line between her brows. "*Very* unfortunate. I've made a bit of a study of the shards in the last couple of years, and I have to say that the whole business seems to depend on very strict timing. How have you trained? Ywain's daughter you may be, but if you haven't been trained sufficiently before you try to seal up the land, it will probably do more harm than good to give you the shards."

"*Shards?*" Dion, startled and joyful, knew a fierce relief. There wasn't one more shard to find: Montalier had the last two! "You have more than one!"

Althea looked at Markon. He looked back at her and shrugged. "I'd like it to be remembered for posterity that I wasn't the one who gave it away."

Althea, with great dignity, said: "I wasn't trying to keep it a secret. Dion has every right to know where the shards are. Do you have all the others?"

"Yes," Dion said, nodding. It didn't occur to her to hide anything from Althea. "We have all but your two."

Markon folded his arms across his chest in interest. "Who is *we?*"

"There are seven of us. Two humans, two Fae, one Guardian, and two...well, I'm not sure if they're dragon or human, actually."

"Speaking hypothetically," said Althea slowly; "what else would you need if we were to give you the last two shards? How do you intend to rejoin the blade?"

"We'd need the use of a forge. We bought our own blacksmith with us–"

"Coinnach's son as well? Goodness me!"

"And I've been training since I was a child," Dion added. Althea's doubts had stung a little, despite Dion's own insecurities.

Althea looked decidedly speculative. "Alawn's daughter taught how to bind Faery? How did that come about?"

"One of the Guardians taught me. He's– well, I've known him for quite a while now."

"Oh, this just keeps getting more interesting!" cried Althea. "I can't do anything with the shards, you see; it's this Fae magic of mine. Not at all compatible. Well, you'd better invite the rest of your group in: I'm sure we can find somewhere for them all."

"*Invite*– well– they're–"

Markon, taking pity on her, said: "I think what Dion is trying to say is that the rest of her desperate ruffians are just outside the window in the other room."

"They might as well come through the window, then," said Althea practically. "It'll be quicker than going around by the front entrance, anyway. You'll have to tell me all about how you got past our security, by the way. I think Sal will be very interested to know about our gaping holes in security."

"Well, that's one way of putting it," said Markon, starting across the room. Dion instinctively froze, and though she immediately flushed and corrected the rigidity of her stance, Markon slowed his pace. "Will you lead the way, or shall I?"

Ashamed of herself, Dion said: "I'd better. Barric will be worried if he doesn't see me first." She turned her back on them very deliberately: it would have been rude in any other context, but she was quite sure that Althea and Markon would see it for the expression of trust that it was. The rooms didn't seem quite so large or so dangerous now that they was gently lit, and Dion was back at the window in mere moments. She jumped herself up onto the windowsill, half in and half out, and looked around anxiously.

"Barric?"

"I'm here."

"We've been invited in."

Barric stared at her, a line between his brows; then nodded. He disappeared back into the shadows, and Dion opened the larger, lower part of the window in readiness. A moment later Kako trod lightly along the ledge, Rafiq a dark shadow close behind her. She nodded at Althea and Markon as she slipped through the window, entirely at her ease. The king and queen took the invasion with unimpaired good humour, but when Carmine entered the room with a cheerfully irreverent: "What a delightful surprise for you! Isn't it nice to see me again?" there was a noticeable stillness to the air. Dion saw Althea stiffen and Markon frown; but as Althea's eyes travelled over Fancy, she smiled suddenly and said: "You're keeping better company of late, Carmine."

"I always keep good company," said Carmine, making way for Fancy. He gave Fancy a glinting, flirtatious smile and added: "But it seems to be getting better and better, I'll admit."

Markon, his frown quickly dissolving into deep amusement, said: "Lady Halme, I believe? We met several years ago."

"That's right," said Fancy. "I was trying to break Parrin's curse."

"You're the one Carmine wouldn't give up," said Althea, her smile growing. "Carmine, you sneaky, slithery Fae!"

"That's no way to talk to an old friend," Carmine said. "I'd offer to kiss you but I'm not certain your husband wouldn't hit me, and I *know* Fancy would."

"Do you mean to say that you knew the king and queen after all that?" demanded Padraig indignantly. "What do you mean by making us sneak about through windows and over roofs?"

"The sheer fun of it all," said Carmine. "They stole something from me once and I wanted to repay the favour."

"Now *that*, I want to hear about," said Padraig. "What did you steal from him, your majesties?"

"I'm beginning to wonder that myself," Markon said ruefully. "I'm beginning to have the feeling that we never stole it at all."

Althea, serenely closing the window behind everyone, said: "It's a long story and the princess is tired. We'll talk about it tomorrow after you've all slept."

AFTER THEY'D *slept* turned out to mean the next evening when everyone finally gathered together again in a large library equidistant from their various rooms. Kako and Rafiq had been with Markon's steward Sal all afternoon, their wingspan frequently seen over the battlements and widow's walks as they showed him the holes in his security. Fancy and Carmine were also out of sight for most of the day, and when Barric appeared again he smelled of fire and forge. Dion had the impression that he had been preparing Althea and Markon's forge for the reforging that was to happen early tomorrow.

Dion herself spent an entirely delightful day with Padraig, bullying him in the pleasantest way imaginable to lie down on one of the settees in the library and allow her to check on his healing wound. Their ideas on how Padraig should heal were wildly different, but since Padraig's idea of healing was to pull her down on the settee beside him and kiss her until she was breathless, Dion didn't object as much as she thought she ought to. They were interrupted by Barric in a quiet moment, and though he would have pulled back out of the room, he was followed so quickly by Althea that he returned with a slight smile. Althea situated herself somewhat carefully on a fat, velvety chair and seemed determined to strike up a conversation with Dion, while Barric sat in a corner and methodically went over his blades and sheaths. He was always inclined to regularly check his gear, but Dion had the impression that he was deliberately withdrawing from the company.

They were very soon joined by the rest of their company, who besides an air of frivolity and hilarity, brought with them an assortment of tiny pies and an inclination to discuss the mythos behind the Broken Sword.

"My people have an old legend that says the original forgers broke the Sword in pieces to keep it better hidden from the Fae," said Rafiq, in one of his rare moments of speech.

"That's not entirely correct," said Althea. *"The Song of the Broken Sword* never comes right out and says it, but I think the original makers weren't as inclined to give up their lives, willy-nilly. I think they tried to get around the life-giving bit by joining together and each giving a good bit of their own magic to bind Faery. That's what split the Sword, if I'm right. It's just a theory, mind. Now the *reforging–*"

"It's a good theory," said Barric. He was sharpening his sword with a steady, regular rhythm of whetstone against iron, and the sudden cessation of noise seemed to startle the company as much as his sudden speaking. "It's the truth."

Althea looked at him speculatively, and Dion thought that two questions seemed to vie for precedence. At last, with a half-glance in Dion's direction, the enchantress said: "Were you there, then?"

"No," said Barric, and went back to his sharpening. "But I knew someone who was."

"I see," said Althea. "I'm a little curious about the reforging, however. Perhaps you could–"

Padraig, from his seat beside Dion, said: "What a thing to be speaking of! We've enough dole to last us until next winter, and the Sword is to be reforged tomorrow. Let's be merry and enjoy our night."

"Enjoy?" asked Althea, her eyes flickering from Padraig to Dion. She was frowning, and Dion had the feeling that she was distinctly disapproving. "I must say that I'm a little confused. I'd thought the reforging to be more of a draining kind of–"

Padraig's eyes met hers rather convulsively, and Althea

stopped short, her frown more pronounced. Dion saw it and felt the sharp clutch of discomfort: she hated hidden words and secret meanings, now more than ever. She said abruptly: "I'm going to sleep," and left them to their secrets and hidden meanings.

Her annoyance had worn off by the time she got back to her room. Her mellowing was due in a large part to the fact that now the shards of the Broken Sword were together again, her death approached in all its calming certainty. It was hard to be distracted by petty annoyances when something so important stood in comparison with them. It was also, thought Dion, smiling slightly, very hard to remain annoyed with someone so consistently delightful as Padraig.

She flopped on her bed and gazed up at the cream-coloured mouldings that ran around the ceiling, enjoying the silence of the evening. She didn't realise she'd fallen asleep until a loud rattle at her window-casement woke her with a start. Dion froze, her heart pounding loud in her ears, and heard the clatter again. She crept from her bed, spilling the duvet onto the rug, and was just wondering rather wildly if she should scream for Barric or simply fling open her window in the hope that it would dislodge the murderer and send him plummeting to his death, when she distinctly heard a voice say: "Hist! Cherry! You've never gone to sleep, have you?"

"Padraig!" Dion hurried to the window and opened it to find him on the narrow balcony outside. His eyes were glittering and wild, with more than a touch of the Unseelie about them. "What are you doing out there?"

"My balcony joins with yours," he said. "And the big man's door is opposite mine in the hall. I didn't fancy sneaking past his door to get to yours, so here I am! I've come to take you out for the night, cherry!"

"We can't!" protested Dion. "You're supposed to be reforging the Sword tomorrow: you should be sleeping."

"No time to waste," sang Padraig, waltzing toward her and sweeping her across the floorboards to a tune that only he could hear. "No time to waste, my darling cherry! We're to be married, sure!"

Dion, swept irresistibly toward the window, found herself laughing. "We can't get married!"

"We can," said Padraig, and kissed her. "We will!" He kissed her again. "What's the matter, cherry; don't you want to marry me?"

Dion looked into those bright, entreating eyes and said without hesitation: "Yes. Oh yes! But don't you want a Fae bonding ceremony? We can have it after you've reforged the Sword, with everyone there."

"I don't want everyone there," said Padraig, dragging her out through the window. "I only want you. And I don't want to wait."

Dion, catching his bubbling brightness, was bundled across the balcony into Padraig's room and out of his door, after much giggling and many suspicious looks up and down the corridor. They ran through the castle hand in hand as if they were a pair of children, attracting amused looks from the few servants they met with and a decidedly disapproving look from the stiff individual who let them out into the courtyard and arranged for a small, sleek carriage to take them into the city streets beyond the castle wall.

"Well now," said Padraig, pulling Dion close to him in the carriage. "There's meant to be a wedding-band. We'll have to fix that."

"I don't need a bracelet," Dion said, laughing. Padraig paid as little attention to that as he had to her protestations that he should be sleeping, and leapt from the slowly-moving carriage as it rolled smoothly through a brightly-lit night market that crossed several streets and filled the air with the mingled scents of various Montalieran specialty pies. The carriage slowed as the driver caught sight of Padraig's antics, but by the time it stopped he had vaulted eagerly back in, kissing Dion with breathless abandon. When he had made Dion as breathless as he was, he knelt on the carriage floor and presented the fruits of his escapade: a child's bauble with bright glass beads in peacock colours. It was nothing like a proper wedding band, but Dion put out her hand unhesitatingly for Padraig to clasp it around her wrist.

He said: "Marry me, cherry?"

"Yes," Dion said simply. "But where's your band?"

"Ah, it's a pretty thing!" said Padraig, his eyes dancing as he slid back into the seat beside her. "Here you go, cherry!"

Dion took it and bubbled over with laughter again. Padraig's band was just as bright and childish as her own; nothing like the plain, masculine thing a groom's band usually was. She slipped it onto his wrist anyway, kissing his palm. That pleased Padraig so much that it was quite some time before they had leisure to look out the windows again in search of either a Watch Station or a sign that indicated an Officiator of the Court.

When they were again attending to their surroundings, it was Dion who said eagerly: "There! A Watch Station!" and pulled on the bell-cord to stop the carriage. They bowled to a stop before a flight of stone stairs that climbed to the entrance of a tidy Watch Station, well-lit and cheerful. Dion was spun out of the carriage, clinging tight to Padraig's shoulders, and laughed her joy to the starry sky above.

"Onward and upward!" said Padraig, as bright and glittering as the stars. They danced up the stairs together, Dion breathless with laughter and wondering if it was possible that they were both drunk on the night air.

The door was opened to them by a Watch Captain with an off-putting likeness to Duc Owain ap Rees and a stern, honest look that managed to bring a touch of solemnity to both Dion and Padraig without quenching their joy. He married them in his sensible, tidy office, then sent them off again with a piece of paper testifying to the fact and a small apricot pie that must have been his dinner, judging by the touch of regret that Dion saw in his eyes. She kissed his cheek in passing, delighting in his instant gruffness, and was dragged off by Padraig.

"I'll not have my wife kissing other men," he said firmly.

Dion had given up wondering what hour it was by the time they sneaked back into Padraig's room. They had wandered through another street market, danced in a tiny corner-eatery where the music was fast and the tables open to the night air, and eaten their pie under the stars with their feet in a fountain dedicated to some long-dead Montalieran heroine before returning to the castle.

"The nicest wedding I've ever attended," said Padraig, kissing Dion below her left ear. "Mm, you smell like apricots, cherry."

"So do you," objected Dion, both surprised and disappointed to find that Padraig was dancing her back out to the balcony and into her own room.

"Not a complaint," murmured Padraig, his lips grazing her ear. Dion sat down rather suddenly on the bed, breathless and weak in the most pleasant way imaginable. "I hope you don't mind, cherry, but I'd much rather not spend my wedding night alone."

"Nor would I," said Dion, watching with fascinated eyes as Padraig's nimble fingers unbuttoned his shirt. "I thought you were going to put me to bed."

"Aye, and so I am," said Padraig.

DION WOKE WITH A SMILE, a feeling of unaccustomed lightness buoying her heart. She had woken briefly early in the morning to find Padraig beside her, his arms possessively around her and one ankle hooked with hers. He had kissed her in his sleep, clumsy and warm, and Dion had drifted back off to sleep with the entirely contented feeling that she could die happily tomorrow.

When she woke again he was gone, and sunlight was edging the curtains. Dion had a moment of lazy happiness to stretch and admire her bright wedding band before it occurred to her that she had slept much later than she meant to. Both sets of curtains had been drawn to shut out the light, possibly by Padraig when he left. Moreover, Dion had woken only because someone was tapping at the door. She tumbled out of bed, scrambling to find her borrowed dressing-robe, and opened the door to Althea's worried face.

"You'd better get dressed," said the queen. Her eyes fell on the gaudy wedding-band that sat below the sleeve of Dion's robe, and widened a little. "Oh dear. Have I been mistaken? Has he already told you?"

"Told me what?" Dion's stomach had taken on the fluttering consistency of a swarm of butterflies.

Althea looked slightly annoyed with herself. "No, of course not. You wouldn't still be here if he had. You'd best get down to the forge as quickly as possible, then: they've already started."

"The reforging?" Dion stared at her. "Why would they start without me?"

"Get dressed," said Althea, her face set and stern. Dion did as she was told this time, shrugging into her clothes from the day before. The queen, entirely unembarrassed at her nakedness, said: "I take it that no one has explained to you exactly what happens when a Fae uses up *all* of their magic?"

"No," said Dion, her tones laced with dismay. "But– but Padraig has his hammer and anvil–"

"–which he ensorcelled with his own magic," said Althea. "Every last drop but the bit that binds them to his will, I suspect. I shouldn't bother to do your hair if I were you. You'll need to be as quick as possible if you want to see your husband before he dies."

"No!" said Dion, dashing after Althea. The queen was a swift walker despite her pregnancy. "No! It can't be true! *I'm* the one who will die: Padraig was just to give up his magic!"

"That's what you don't understand," said Althea grimly. "For a Fae, to give up their magic *is* to die!"

Never had a journey of ten minutes seemed so like ten hours. Dion, now far outpacing Althea in a desperate sprint for the castle's forge, felt as though the world moved in slow motion around her. The halls were a darkened maze, the castle courtyard a blinding confusion of light; and when she at last saw the door to the forge, she could feel the cool essence of Unseelie night flowing from it despite the fact that it was bright morning. There was a darkness of magic at the door: Dion plunged into it, following the sound of hammer against anvil, and found herself in a room that flickered with white flame.

For the first time she saw Padraig in all his Unseelie beauty. His hammer and anvil worked themselves, glowing impossibly with moonlight and sending off starry sparks as hammer struck sword and anvil. Padraig himself, dipped in shadows and touched by moonlight, circled them at a prowl, his eyes on the work and a faint smile of satisfaction that was equal parts light and dark. He sensed her at once, and when his eyes met hers Dion had no doubt that he knew he was to die, and that he wouldn't turn back.

"You shouldn't be here, cherry," he said.

"Please," Dion said, and stopped. It would be treason against Llassar to finish the plea– treason against her whole kind. She could feel the hot tears running down her face, and a numbness creeping up her legs. Barric was there a moment later, a stirring in the air behind her that held her up effortlessly.

Padraig, his blue eyes steady, said: "What, cherry? Are you permitted to give your life for your people while I must not?"

"No," whispered Dion. "I'm sorry. I wish you'd told me."

"How could I? I knew you'd not long to live yourself, and why should you be made unhappy when I could make you happy?"

Dion smiled through her tears. "You made me very happy."

"Well now, that's all an Unseelie outcast could ever hope for," said Padraig, his eyes bright and tender. "I love you, cherry."

"I love you, too."

Padraig looked behind him at the hammer and anvil, hard at work. "It's time to finish the work," he said; and Dion could see that the sword was complete again. It luminesced with the same pale fire in which it had been reforged, the dividing lines between pieces glowing briefly and then fading until it was one gleaming, unblemished whole. Deeper than the metallic surface was the magic that had once been Padraig's; subtle, soft black, against which the scarlet of his destiny-thread showed bright when he bound the reforging together. Dion was watching at the moment he tied the last knot and the destiny-thread became one unbroken band. Padraig's hammer and anvil grew dull– dead, empty metal, as they must once have been before he brought them to life with his magic.

"It's done," he said, and the words were a whisper of leaf against leaf in the moonlight. He turned, and Dion saw the last brightness of his eyes—or was it the gleam of moonlight on leaves?—as he walked once more toward her, one hand outstretched. She reached out to catch that hand and for an instant felt the warmth of flesh; then she was holding leaves and loam, Padraig's wedding band glittering amidst them. Across the floor of the forge, leaves tumbled and scurried as if in a gentle breeze. Moonlight and stars alike were gone: the forge glowed with only the dull remains of a fire.

4

THE FIRST SPRING OF HOPE

*I*f only they had known, thought Dion; and smiled sadly. It was becoming something of a mantra in her life. If only she had known the Fae weren't to be trusted. If only she had known her parents and Aerwn a little better. If only she had known that Padraig was to die.

If only they had known just how many Fae were on the borders of Montalier– or already in Montalier, if it came to that. And if only they had known that reforging the Broken Sword would bring down that furious horde of Fae on their heads before the day was half spent...

They just barely escaped from Montalier as the soft morning turned to warm noon, but they left behind them a kingdom besieged. Althea and Markon had sent them on their way as soon as the first skirmishes were reported, and when Kako and Rafiq sailed too close to the ground over the Avernsian border, such a hail of arrows and magic were directed at them that it took all of Dion's hastily spun defensive spells and all of Kako and Rafiq's terrifyingly quick aerial manoeuvres to avoid them. Barric took an arrow to the upper arm in bundling Dion tightly between himself and Rafiq but the others escaped injury, even the dragons. When Dion tried to call for a halt to take care of Barric's arm he refused to allow the time, and she was forced to turn sideways on Rafiq's huge back with one leg hooked achingly tight around a scaly spine so that she could attend to the injury herself.

"Don't," said Barric, removing her hand when she tried to heal the wound. "You'll need all the energy you can conserve. Wrap it tight and forget about it."

"*I don't want you to die!*" said Dion fiercely.

"It's not my death that should concern you," said Barric; but it did, because he was the only precious thing left that Dion could still cling to. Aerwn, as near to Dion's heart as she was, was half a continent away, and Padraig– Padraig was even further out of reach than that.

They sped high on the breeze and buffeted between clouds, until Dion said suddenly: "Here! We need to stop here!" She felt it with certainty: this was where Faery was to be sealed away from the world of men. This was where the Broken Sword had once been forged, and where it had been broken.

The Fae are following close, said Rafiq's troubled voice. Fancy and Carmine, who must have been speaking with Kako, looked across the void at Dion and nodded.

"As quick as you can, then," said Barric, and Dion saw that he was not the only one checking his knives and loosening his sword in the scabbard. Fancy, her legs edging back to grip Carmine's at the ankle, was also methodically checking her weapons. Carmine sent a bright spit of crimson magic arcing high across the void between them, and smiled such a dark, deadly smile at Dion that she caught her breath and wondered how she could ever have thought Fancy the more dangerous of the two. Rafiq turned his nose toward the swiftly moving grass and began to descend in a stomach-churning dive.

The grass came up to meet them as quickly and inevitably as Dion's doom, and they charged through the long stalks, sending leaf blades and flowers flying in an explosion of green and pink.

Barric leapt for the ground before Rafiq had even slowed and caught Dion as she followed him.

"Where?" he said, panting.

"This way," Dion said; and, seizing his huge hand in her own, she ran for the fold in the land directly ahead. It was deep but narrow, and the hill that rose beyond it rose both in the world of men and in Faery.

"We'll give you as long as we can," called Fancy. Dion, her heart thundering in her ears, half-turned and raised her hand in a last goodbye; or perhaps it was a salute. She wished she could have stopped and said goodbye properly, but even as she and Barric ran for the entrance into Faery, Rafiq and Kako took to the air again, their battle-colours dark against the pink of the late afternoon sky.

Dion and Barric leaped the boundary together, quick and breathless, and Dion stopped dead as she found the world changed and alien around her. Beside her, Barric seemed to let all his breath out in a sigh of home-coming, his fingers curling through hers to grip tight for an instant. He released her hand again almost immediately, and said: "Here?"

"I don't know," said Dion, and there was a tremble in her voice that wasn't from lack of breath. She drew the Broken Sword clumsily from its makeshift scabbard, its leather grip tacky against her palm, and tried to bring back the clarity of sense she had had when in the air.

There was nothing. No guiding light, no certainty of purpose. Here she was, standing in Faery, where the sun wasn't quite warm and the breeze didn't quite touch the skin, the Broken Sword reforged in her hands—Ywain's daughter, come to seal the land, as prophecy foretold—and Dion had not idea of where she was supposed to be or how the Binding was to be begun. Her eyes lifted beyond the sword to where Rafiq and Kako spun and dived in the air; behind them the vast company of Fae that had been following hot on their heels, and before them the very meagre protection of Carmine and Fancy. She could see Fancy's knives glinting in the sunshine, reflecting back Carmine's scarlet storm of magic as it rolled down to meet the approaching Fae.

"Barric–"

He moved until he was in front of her, blocking the sight. "Put it from your mind. You were made for this day. The Sword was made for you."

Dion, as she had done so many times when nothing seemed to make sense, went back to the simplicity of the magic itself. Barric had taught her that. He had taught her that and so much more. She studied the magic of the Sword: its components, its rhythms, its patterns, and its purpose. And deep inside herself she felt the tugging of her own destiny-cord where it nestled within her soul.

"It's time," said Barric; and Dion was so deep in the rhythms of the Sword that she didn't recognise the rhythm of rough-edged sorrow to his voice. She thought of Aerwn—of their parents—and most of all, of Padraig. It was time. Time to be gone; time to go home. Time to join Padraig in the whispering silence of death.

She adjusted her grip on the Sword and let herself relax into its overwhelmingly strong magic. Her first impression was one of incredible vastness: as if her eyes had been opened to see worlds that had been there all along, but were far too massive for her comprehension. Dion saw Avernse spread before her, and considered it all. Then she moved beyond Avernse to Montalier, where the castle was under siege, stopping for a fleeting view of Markon and Althea as they stood hand in hand. Dion let the world move on again, her sights on Llassar and Aerwn, and for a brief, unsatisfactory moment saw her sister and Owain ap Rees fighting furiously back to back amidst a throng of Fae.

"Aerwn!" she gasped. She hauled herself grimly back through Shinpo, desperate to complete the Binding. There was the over-taken Shinpoan castle: there was a young boy, so similar to Kako, desperately fleeing a Fae pursuer through hidden passages and magical byways; an older girl anxiously waiting for him; the imprisoned family they were trying desperately to rescue. She left them behind, seeking Avernse.

It took Dion some time to realise that she was already in Avernse: that she had always been in Avernse. Her sight had telescoped, and now that she could refocus, she saw something else. Before her was a vast host of bright lights, spread throughout the human world; behind her, a still larger host that dwarfed it many times over. Dion exhaled in wonder. She was seeing Fae-lights: the very essence of each and every Fae in both Faery and the human world. The Sword knew them all– could reach them all.

I can kill them, she thought, almost dizzy with the idea of it. *I can kill them all. None of them would ever kill or enslave another human.*

The Fae company far below her shivered and stopped in the midst of the fight. She felt their attention quivering on her; caught and frightened, and all too aware that they could be sealed away from their homeland or slain in an instant. For just one moment Dion felt that she really could kill them all. But there was still that one Fae-light glowing strong directly in front of her human body; and further on was a crimson one that grew in hope as the other Fae-lights around it sank in fear and quivered.

And Dion found that she knew what she had to do next. She reached out to every one of the Fae-lights and sank claws into them with the desperate call of *Now or too late.* Then she sliced through every barrier between Faery and the human world in one decisive motion of the Broken Sword; an open invitation. She saw the Fae-lights brighten—saw the battle line in Llassar waver and then disintegrate; saw a young boy in Shinpo flop to the floor in relief as his Fae attacker disappeared; heard a vague echo of Carmine's victory cry as the Fae host around him forgot about fighting and rippled like a flood across the hills for the closest Faery/human boundary—she saw it all in a moment.

She watched Aerwn and Owain ap Rees on the battlefield,

laughing and bright-eyed as their soldiers roared in joy around them. She wished, for a brief, traitorous moment, that she could be present with Aerwn one last time. Embrace her and say a proper goodbye. But there was no time: Fae-lights were winking out of the human world and into Faery every second, and soon there was only one left. Dion brought her sight back in closer to her body's location, where Rafiq and Kako glided to meet the others on the ground, sweeping through grass that steamed a little as it met their scales. Dion smiled gladly to see them unscathed, and wondered that she could still think in terms of smiling at all. She saw her body smile as if in sleep, and they both laughed softly together. She joined briefly with her body again, feeling the weight of it as a burden, and stood with Barric supporting her.

Ahead of her was the crimson Fae-light, somehow still visible and winking bright on Carmine's forehead. "You'd better come in now," said Dion, the words heavy and unfamiliar in her mouth. "I'm about to seal the border. If you stay there you'll be caught."

"Oh, I'm already caught," said Carmine. It looked as though he merely whisked away a stray hair that fell across his forehead, but his Fae-light was between his fingers the next moment, and he dropped to his knees with the effort of magic.

Fancy fell to her knees beside him, her face white. "Don't! Not for me!"

"Never for you," Carmine gasped, clinging to her hand. "I'm a selfish being and I won't have it said that I stayed for anyone's sake but my own! Take it, Dion ferch Ywain. I don't want it. I have all that I need here."

Dion took it from him and it tickled across her arm until it sat on her forehead, whispering nonsense to her eyebrows.

"Oh, the wrinkles!" said Carmine woefully. "I can feel them forming already."

Fancy snorted a wet laugh into his shoulder and clung to him. "You never looked so pretty," she said.

Dion readjusted her grip on the Sword, and was distantly pleased to find that her hands were neither sweaty nor shaking. "It's time," she said. To Kako she added: "Your family are safe. I've seen them."

Rafiq and Kako didn't shift from their dragon forms, but they made a dragonish obeisance amidst the crackling of grass. *Thank you*, said Kako's voice. *For that– and for other things. It's been an honour.*

This time it was Dion who bowed. She said almost formally: "The honour was mine. And– and thank you. Barric, we need to move further in. I don't want to be caught half way."

Barric lifted her bodily, the Sword resting against his shoulder but still firmly gripped in Dion's white-knuckled fingers. He bowed to the assembled group; and turning his back, he carried Dion further in and further up. She delighted for one last time in the touch of breeze—how she could feel the Faery breeze now that Carmine's Fae-light rested on her forehead!—and revelled in the heat of the day, Faery sun though it was. She ducked her head once more to rest on Barric's shoulder, sighing at the familiar warmth and scent of him, and said: "Just here, Barric."

Barric set her down gently in the leaves and she saw that the others hadn't left: they watched from beyond the fold that spanned Faery and the human world. They were standing witness, their faces upturned to gaze into Faery as long as they could see it. Dion drove the Sword into the ground and felt it join with the Faery earth, sending a network of Binding into the soil deep beneath their feet and spreading high above them into the sky. She smiled at Barric one last time, feeling the heaviness of mortality leave her, and slipped out of her body in a joyful rush to join with the Binding that grew around them. The barriers between Faery and the human world rose swiftly, stronger than ever before; a vast, root-like network of magic that flexed and grew as it knit around Faery. She spared a look for her body and saw it crumpled in Barric's arms, his shoulders bowed and heaving as tears fell silently down his scarred face. Dion found that she could still feel regret, and for a moment wished she had the use of her human body again, just to cling to Barric once more and tell him that it was all right. But the Binding waited, empty and hollow, and she didn't dare to leave her attention divided. In its hollowness Dion seemed to sense a purpose. She gazed at the network of magic that surrounded Faery and found it incomplete: it was only half a spell, a honeycomb of empty spaces and hollow areas that needed to be filled. Into that honeycomb of empty spaces Dion poured her magic; her life; her *self*. She sank into the spell, filling every empty space and incomplete piece, and was astonished at how much of her there was. She was bigger and fuller and so much more alive than she had ever thought.

When Dion had filled the Binding to the brim, her grip on Faery all-consuming and complete, she searched within herself for the crimson dash of destiny that she had seen in Padraig's hammer and anvil. It was the only thing she had been really sure of when it came to binding the land, and it came to her willing and ready, the ethereal ends of it snaking up and around and through every part of the binding. She caught a brief glimpse of her body again; saw the redness that blossomed around its wrists and bound them to the sword. And when, following Padraig's example, she tied the returning ends of the cord together, they knit together until there was no beginning and no end. There was just Dion and the Binding; and Dion *was* the Binding. She found herself wearier than she had ever been, the weight of the Binding heavy on her shoulders. That was ridiculous, of course; because she *had* no shoulders here and there was no real weight. Yet she found herself being compressed and pushed back toward her body by that weight.

No, Dion thought, shocked. *No*. It wasn't meant to be like this. She was meant to die. She was ready to die. She *wanted* to die. Why wasn't the Sword letting her die? She flowed through the scarlet thread of destiny that bound her to the Sword, searching desperately for wrong ties and missing threads, but found it unfrayed and wholly binding. It was then that she understood, in a terrible clarity of knowledge. The Binding didn't want her death; it wanted her life. Aerwn had been almost right: the Binding was Dion and Dion was the Binding, but Dion would live in spite of it. And while she lived, Faery would be bound.

There was an ache in Dion's heart, and somewhere at the back of her consciousness something was still tugging, *tugging*. A heavy certainty dragged her down; back to the ground and back to her body. Dion was thrown back into her body with a painful thump, gasping and struggling, and found herself looking up into Barric's stunned eyes. They stared at each other until Barric's scar stretched and he laughed huskily through his tears.

"Dion," he said, his voice weary and curiously satisfied. And then again: "Dion."

Dion's face crumpled. "It doesn't want my death," she said. There was still a terrible aching in her heart. She could have died without Padraig, but how was she supposed to live without him? "It doesn't want my death, Barric: it wants my *life*."

Barric pulled her close and Dion clung around his neck, her face buried in his shoulder. "It wasn't meant to be like this!" she wept. "I was supposed to die! He was supposed to live and I was supposed to die!"

Barric held her in silence until she ceased to cry, and then for some time longer after that. When Dion had cried herself out she simply sat where she was, clutching wrists that were still scarlet-bound in a physical reminder that she herself was now as much the Broken Sword as the Sword itself. The two wedding-bands that were on her left wrist—hers and Padraig's—had seamlessly joined with the binding, bright bubbles of contrasting colour in the smooth red. Dion knew without tugging at them that she would never be able to remove them, but she ran her fingers over them anyway. They were smooth and light.

"We'll have to find somewhere safe to keep the Sword," she said at last. "It's not– well, I don't think it's breakable, but just in case."

Barric nodded. "There's a place ready. Careful." He caught her as she tried to stand and found that she wasn't quite steady. Dion gripped his arm with one hand and pulled the Broken Sword from the ground with the other. It didn't feel as heavy as it had felt before, and it slid back into its scabbard as smoothly as if she had carried it all her life. "I'll speak with the other Guardians. See if there's a way of getting you back to the human world."

Dion tried to laugh, but it came out as more of a sob. "There isn't," she said. "I can't go back. Even if there *was* a way I couldn't. If I leave Faery, the Sword will break again and the borders will begin to fall."

"Then we'll find somewhere safe for you as well," said Barric. He took her hand; and Dion, feeling the dappled warmth of Faery sunshine on her face, allowed herself to be led through the trees and into her new life.

5

THE TURNING OF THE SEASON

*A*erwn ferch Pobl had been queen for five years before she brought herself to enter her sister's suite once again. She wasn't sentimental, but the loss of her twin had cut deeply, and even Owain ap Rees' strongly worded criticisms hadn't been enough to break the seal on a door that held only sorrow within.

Nor did she mean to enter the suite again when she did. It was a spur-of-the-moment decision—as quite often happened with Aerwn—and had she not been passing by Dion's closed-up suite on the way to her own old suite, it may never have been made. But she did find herself there late one afternoon, passing the royal seal that closed up Dion's door; and Aerwn had never been one to back away from a forbidden thing, even if she was the one who had forbidden it. On a whim, she drew her ceremonial dagger and flicked away the seal, turning the door-knob before it could occur to her to turn back. She found herself amidst cobwebs and ghostly dust-covers, her footsteps sending up puffs of dust as she walked a path she had often walked, years ago. Back then, Aerwn would have thrown herself on the bed and waited for Dion to finish dressing. Her sister would nervously check her appearance in the mirror–

That mirror! thought Aerwn, startled. It was still there. She had all but forgotten it: the window into Faery that had brought Dion to her doom. It occurred to Aerwn that if she could just *see* Barric, she would give him a proper piece of her mind. She tore the dust-cover from the mirror, sending dust and cobwebs into the air in choking cloud, and for an eye-watering moment was too busy coughing and sneezing in tandem to pay attention to anything else. She wiped her streaming eyes, and thought she heard Dion's voice saying: "Aerwn?"

Aerwn looked up wildly. A familiar, startled face looked back at her from the mirror, and she was crushed by a ridiculous disappointment until it occurred to her that the room in the mirror was not the one in which she stood– the long, loose, curling hair around the face in the mirror not her own short-cropped curls.

"Dion!" she gasped. "Dion!"

"Finally!" said Dion, her eyes luminous with bright, happy tears. "Oh, finally! Aerwn, you have no idea how long I've waited to see you!"

"You're dead," said Aerwn, sitting down rather suddenly on the bed. "You're *not* dead! How are you not dead? And who are *they*?"

She saw the flush rise to Dion's face as easily as it had ever risen, and looked past her sister again to the two children who were playing behind her. The girl—a quick, pale-skinned thing with dark curls just like Dion's and a pair of blue eyes that could only have come from Padraig—gave her a swift, uninterested look and went back to her window, but the younger child's eyes were fastened on Aerwn and had been for some time. He was a solemn, fat, little thing with dark, smooth skin and wide grey eyes that looked impassively at his aunt. Aerwn, who had been unnerved more than once by the same gaze from Barric, gaped.

"Dion ferch Ywain, what *have* you been getting up to?"

Dion, still very pink, allowed the smaller child to climb into her lap and curled her arms around him while he continued to stare unblinkingly at Aerwn. "I got married."

"Yes!" spluttered Aerwn. "I gathered that!"

"Actually, I seem to have um, got married twice," admitted her sister, the colour deepening in her cheeks. "It's a long story."

Aerwn threw back her head and laughed. "Yes! Five years long!" She wriggled back on the mildewed bed-covers as if no time at all had passed; as if it was just she and Dion talking before court sessions again. "I'm comfortable. Take your time."

6

BONUS SCENE!

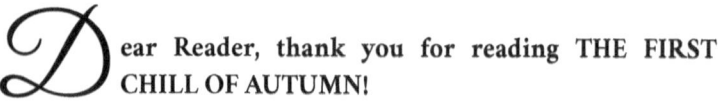ear Reader, thank you for reading THE FIRST CHILL OF AUTUMN!

BELOW IS A SPECIAL SCENE FOR THOSE OF YOU WHO (LIKE SOME OF MY BETA READERS) NEED SOME KIND OF CLOSURE FOR DION AND BARRIC.

THE SILENCE WAS PERHAPS the thing Dion most loved about Faery. Not the silence of bird and beast, but the lack of babble; of human rush and tumble; of confusion. Like Barric's silence, it was calming and precious. Dion had been in Faery three years, and the peace of it still caught her by surprise. Barric had brought her high into the mountains of Faery shortly after the Binding, their journey sober and silent through the whispering forest. Dion, her scarlet bands tough and light, had walked beside him; lifted over tree-trunks and tossed up high, steep embankments as the wind grew colder and more incisive. And when they arrived at a grim, stone mountain-face, he had opened an impossible stone door at the base of it and ushered her into a steep corridor of stairs.

There was a castle hidden in the mountain, its ramparts the jagged stone and its turrets the rocky outcrops. In Dion's first few months she thought there was only bare stone beyond the beautiful interior, but she was very much confined to the interior for those first few months. First by unexpected sickness and then by a startlingly swelling stomach– which both culminated, a little less than nine months later, in a tiny waif of a girl child with the bluest eyes Dion had ever seen. With her Unseelie heritage it was perhaps unsurprising that little Aoife didn't find nights in Seelie Faery as dark as she would have liked. There were many nights that Dion found herself walking the halls to rock Aoife to sleep beneath the faint gleam of the stars, and as she explored the outdoor walkways and curved parabolas open to the sky, she began to discover the stone carvings that were etched into every part of the castle. Her favourite, a stone eagle taking off into the sweeping void below from a stone pelmet on the balustrade, became the meeting place where she sat with Barric every evening after Aoife finally began to sleep through the night. Together they watched the evening fade from blue-edged pink to dark lavender, which was as close to night as Faery came in its slightly more Seelie environs. Someone had moved a velvet-covered sofa onto the parabola when it was noticed how often Dion stood there, and Barric and Dion shared it; Barric's long legs propped on the stone balustrade and Dion curled up beside him, leaning into his warmth.

They sat so again tonight, Barric's head arched back to catch a glimpse of the faintly glimmering stars and Dion frowning down at her scarlet-bound wrist where her wedding bands glowed softly in the mauve half-light. The season was turning. As high in the mountains as they were, the turn of the season meant heavy snows and many hours indoors before the massive fireplace that was big enough (or so Valance, the dourest of the Guardians Dion had yet met, said) to roast an entire human. The turn of the season also meant that Barric would soon be gone for three months. Dion had begun to dread that time more and more as it approached each year; the day that Barric would be gone once again and the sofa cold and empty beside her. The castle halls were peopled by Guardians and other Fae, but although Dion had made tentative friends with some of them, none of them were quite capable of filling the huge void left by Barric's absence. Even Aoife was unsettled and inclined to whine when Barric was gone, prone to an otherwise unusual irritability. Dion was never exactly sure what it was that Barric did while he was gone: she had the impression that he was still quietly moving things around Faery in accordance with the Guardians' plans. Whatever it was, she grudged the time he spent away from her as bitterly as Aoife did.

The glint of lavender must have caught Barric's eye, because Dion saw his eyes flick down at her wedding bands.

"Do you still think about him?"

Dion's hand dropped at once, tucking beneath the folds of her skirt. She said quietly: "Sometimes." She would very much have preferred Barric not to catch her looking at the bands. Of late there had been a small, delicate idea in the back of her mind that she had curiously examined in the silence and privacy of her own thoughts. It said that Barric was perhaps fonder of her than he had ever acknowledged. Dion, who had known the sudden brilliance of giddy young love with Padraig in a dream long ago, had found herself not quite certain of her own feelings.

No: she was certain of them. But they had grown so softly and slowly, and rooted themselves so deeply in her heart that it had taken her far too long to realise what they were. It occurred to her that perhaps she had been blind for too long; that Barric's continued silence meant he had ceased to hope for more from her than their daily companionship. Over the last few weeks Dion had tried to convey, as clearly as someone so shy *could* convey, that she would welcome more than friendship. She couldn't convince herself that it had had any effect: Barric had been as kind, thoughtful, and gentle as ever, but he hadn't shown any sign of taking advantage of her tentative advances.

It was possible, thought Dion, her thoughts an uncomfortable mix of uncertainty and slight embarrassment, that he hadn't even noticed them. She didn't think she was particularly good at hinting. Or making advances, if it came to that.

She said now: "It's– it's part of me now, but it's not all of me. It doesn't eat away at me anymore." She turned her eyes on him as she spoke, hoping to show him by the clarity of her expression that the past had lost its power to influence her, but Barric's eyes were dwelling meditatively on the stone eagle.

A shadow passed behind them, and Dion, looking instinctively over her shoulder, caught the cold, unfriendly glance of Valance as he passed the stone-hewn window that framed their parabola.

"I don't think Valance approves of me," she said, willing to turn the subject. Valance's disapproval wasn't the gut-wrenching thing it had been when she first arrived in the mountains, but it still made her uncomfortable.

"It's me that Valance doesn't approve of," Barric said coolly. "He doesn't approve of me keeping company with a human. And he doesn't approve of the Broken Sword keeping company with a mere Guardian."

"But–" Dion found herself stifling a giggle. "But that means he'd disapprove no matter what."

Barric nodded, smiling faintly. He seemed preoccupied.

Dion, after a brief moment of silence, said quietly: "I suppose you'll be gone tomorrow?"

"Yes." Barric's eyes met hers for a fleeting moment before they went back to the eagle. "I've arranged something for you while I'm gone."

Dion said curiously: "Arranged?" Barric, as well as failing to acknowledge her advances, had been less present than usual over the last few weeks. Was this what he had been up to?

"I've been trying to resurrect an old piece of magic," he said. "Yesterday, I succeeded. Do you remember the mirror?"

Her gasp was a hint of vapour on the cold air. "You– you made it work again?"

"Your thread of magic was still running through it. If Aerwn is there, you'll be able to talk to her. It's best not to hope too much, but–"

"She'll be there," Dion said, with certainty. If she knew her sister, it would sooner or later occur to Aerwn to put the mirror put into her own chambers on the off chance that one day communications would be resumed with Faery– if only to thoroughly eviscerate Barric verbally for her sister's death.

"It's ready now," he said. "I'm content. Go and see your sister if you can."

Dion looked up at him through her lashes, but didn't move. "When are you leaving? Tonight?"

"Yes," said Barric.

"I'll try to see Aerwn tomorrow," she said. Her heart was beating a slightly faster rhythm. It was now or never; because Barric would be gone tomorrow and if she didn't say it now she would never again have the courage. "Back there," she said, her hand flicking vaguely. She always seemed to call the human world 'back there', as if it wasn't quite real any more. Perhaps it *wasn't* quite real any more. "I told you I loved you."

Barric smiled down at her. "I remember."

Dion drew in a breath, her heart ticking in her ears, faster and faster. "Well, I still do."

"I know," said Barric, his large hand covering hers and pressing gently.

"No, you don't," said Dion, her tongue tied and her face growing warmer. "I mean, it's different. It has been different for a little while now. That is, it– it c-can be different. If– if you want."

Barric, as still as she had ever seen him, didn't reply. Nor did he look up from his rather frozen study of the eagle pelmet when she leaned up to kiss his cheek. Dion stood abruptly, with the sickening thought that she had been entirely mistaken, and hurried away across the parabola to hide her burning face in the welcome shadows of the stone halls.

She didn't hear the step that fell, but she knew the familiar warmth behind her before Barric turned her around, his hands on her shoulders and then cupping her face. His dark eyes were glowing with a soft, triumphant light, his chest rising and falling just a little too quickly. She had seen that look from him before: the day of the Binding, when she had come back from the dead. It was a look that said something else had come back from the dead tonight.

He lowered his head and kissed her, his fingers threaded through her hair, then pulled back to smile at her. "I knew I had to wait, but I didn't know how long. I didn't mean to make you unhappy."

"I thought it had taken me too long to understand," Dion said, her relief bright and warm. "I thought you might not love me anymore."

"I have loved you," he said. "I will love you."

"I've loved you, too," said Dion, her hand rising to touch his cheek. Barric kissed her fingers, his eyes still on her face. "Though I didn't know it until a little while ago."

The night was cool and the velvet of the sofa was warm, and when Barric led her back out onto the parabola, Dion didn't object. They sat together contentedly in the crystal air of Faery night, and she said: "Does this mean you're not leaving tonight?" She couldn't keep the hope from springing up, as vain as she knew it to be.

She saw Barric smile, his eyes warm. "No. It can't be avoided. But I will be quick." He kissed her, sweet and lingering. "I will be *very* quick." Another kiss, and an almost crushing hug. "And when I get back, we will talk."

7

A TALE OF CARMINE & FANCY

Somewhere in the depths of Faery, rather more to the Unseelie than the Seelie, there was a moderately sized castle. Despite its modest size it was about as ostentatiously gilded as is possible for a castle to be whilst retaining some semblance of believability as a fortified dwelling.

In the depths of that castle was an equally ornate suite, and in that suite was a beautiful room with a great, round, starry portal of crystal open to display the perennially moonlit Unseelie Sky. Below the portal was a massive bed with cool silk sheets, a fat swansdown duvet, and more pillows than could possibly be said to be practical. The owner of said castle, suite, room, and bed was fast asleep on top of the duvet as if he'd thrown himself there, careless of the richness of his surroundings.

Within the circle of the room a clock was chiming twelve bells. Despite the chimes, the Fae on the bed showed no signs of stirring, but his stillness now seemed to hold more of an attitude of determined, rather than actual, somnolence. When the last chime had sent its golden tones through the room, the door to the bedroom opened. A tall, straight figure swept through the door in a businesslike manner, her skirts whispering against the floor, and the Fae on the bed stiffened.

"It's time to get up, my lord."

A groan.

"It's no good sulking about it."

Another groan.

"And it's no good refusing to speak, either: I know you're awake."

A tousled head emerged from the depths of the mounded pillows. "Who told you," demanded the lord of the castle, "to wake me up at this disgustingly early hour?"

"Actually, it's past noon," said the lady, her calm unimpaired. "And your visitor told me to wake you. A rather large gentleman with an even larger sword."

The lord's eyes narrowed on her. "I believe I told you to kick Barric out if he ever came back."

"You did, my lord," agreed the lady.

"Then *why* did you let him in?"

"For one thing, he's much bigger than I am," said the lady, with a touch of pink to her cheeks, "and for another, I couldn't get the door closed quickly enough. He told me to tell you to guard your own door next time. Oh, and he mentioned that if you're not down in ten minutes, he's going to come up and fetch you."

She swept to one side, neatly avoiding the lord's frantic leap out of bed, and serenely remained where she was while he frantically searched the cluttered room.

He growled: "*Help* me, Fancy!"

Fancy cleared her throat. "My lord?"

He looked up wildly, his eyes falling on the shirt that dangled by its collar from Fancy's forefinger. "You were hiding that!"

"I don't *have* to hide it," said Fancy. Her eyes flicked up and down his bare chest in a manner sufficiently governess to make the lord's eyes flash dangerously. "You hardly ever wear a shirt:

I'm surprised you even know where they're kept. This one needs washing, by the way."

"How can it need washing if I never wear it?" argued the lord. "It will certainly do for Barric, however. What do you think, Fancy? Shall I comb my hair, or is artfully rumpled a look to be desired?"

"I think that if you're not downstairs in half a minute, Barric will be coming through that door," said Fancy.

The sound of explosive muttering filtered through the lord's shirt as he struggled into it. Fancy didn't so much as blink: she merely held open the door to the suite so that his lordship Carmine Nightshade, lord of Glasslight Canton and Duke of the Wandering Hollies, could stumble through it with his head still stuck in his shirt.

Carmine had managed to emerge from his shirt by the time he reached the grand stairs. That was possibly just as well, since the grand staircase was an exercise in the most whimsical of Fae architecture: a series of floating steps in crystal as clear as the dawn, suspended by nothing and supported by nothing but the most unnoticeable of magics. Still, he paid the treacherous stairs as little heed as if he *had* still been struggling within his shirt, causing Fancy, who was following behind in a much more sedate manner, to flick her eyes toward the ceiling and sigh. No one, looking at Carmine, would have guessed that he had had to be picked up from the bottom of the stairs several times this cycle already. Carmine took very good care that no one did, either. As much as the stairs, was Carmine an exercise in the most whimsy that Faery had to offer.

Now, ignoring the last few steps and leaping lightly down to the main hall, he threw a look that was as wary as it was comprehensive, around white-marbled area.

"Carmine," said a deep voice, in greeting. The door to the drawing room was obscure with shadow. That shadow resolved and solidified into the form of a very large, dark-skinned Fae, the double-grip of his greatsword rising in an inky blot over his left shoulder. He had to duck his head to fit beneath the lintel of the door.

"What have you been doing to my Fancy?" demanded Carmine, trying to pretend he wasn't out of breath. "She was ruffled. Fancy is never ruffled."

"I picked her up," said the other Fae.

"I won't have you picking up my servants willy-nilly," said Carmine. "*Especially* Fancy. She's the only one I've got who has her feet on the ground and I won't have her corrupted."

The other Fae shrugged. "She was in the way and I didn't want to hurt her."

"You didn't have to hold me *quite* so tightly," said Fancy's voice. She was still descending the stairs in a carefully lady-like way.

The huge Fae gave her a considering look that, to Carmine's obvious annoyance, made her blush faintly. "I didn't want you to hurt me, either," he said.

"What do you think she was going to do?" demanded Carmine. "Scold you into submission?"

"Would you care for tea, my lords?" asked Fancy, coming to a deferential halt at the base of the stairs. She seemed not to hear Carmine's remark, but one long finger tapped against her leg where it was hidden in the folds of her skirt.

"Good heavens, no!" said Carmine. "Champagne, of course. Barric?"

"Tea, thank you," said Barric. He bowed to Fancy, and she swept him a brief curtsey in return before disappearing down the great hall.

"What did I *just* tell you about ruffling Fancy?" said Carmine, in annoyance.

Barric merely said: "Are you coming in, or do I have to fetch you?"

"My champagne isn't here yet," complained Carmine. He

sauntered carelessly through the door, but said as he did so: "It's too early in the morning to deal with your disgusting energy without champagne."

"I apologise," Barric said, and shut the door.

It would be incorrect to say that once the door closed, Carmine's demeanour changed completely. His eyes certainly looked more alert, but he threw himself bonelessly onto a ruby-red sofa as if he hadn't a care in the world.

"What's the word, big man?"

"It's time," said Barric.

Carmine shrugged. "Oh well. I knew it was coming, I suppose. What do you need?"

"Do you still have the shard?"

"You ask that as though it's a rhetorical question."

The very air seemed to grow still. Barric said, very quietly: "Do you mean that you do *not* have the shard?"

"Let's be honest, big man," said Carmine. "Is it really something that someone like me should be trusted with?"

"Until now, I'd always thought so. Where is the shard?"

"You can't have thought so," Carmine said. "I told you I wasn't to be trusted. I told you I was being watched. Actually, I thought that the words '*I am not a trustworthy person*' and '*since when does Unseelie help anyone*' were warning enough without my direct refusal to guard the shard. Obviously I was wrong."

"Where is the shard?"

"And now that I come to think of it, I don't know why you brought it to me in the first place. You must have known what I'd say."

"Where. Is. The. Shard?"

"Now, *there's* the rub. I don't know with absolute certainty."

"*Carmine.*"

Carmine still lay at ease on the sofa, but his eyes were watchful. "Don't do anything you'll regret, Big Man."

"I won't regret it," said Barric, and took a step forward.

"Your refreshment, my lords," said a cool voice by the door. Fancy was just slipping through it, her skirts brushing lightly against the wood.

Barric, looking very surprised, said: "How did you open that?"

"That's what I'd like to know, too," agreed Carmine. "She always manages to do that, and I've no idea how. She's not especially magical, you know."

"How much did you hear?"

"I never hear anything unless I'm supposed to hear it," said Fancy. "Will you take a cup, my lord?"

"No," said Barric. "I've something more important to attend to."

Fancy's step wasn't hurried, but she somehow managed to be between Carmine and Barric the next minute, her tray primly in front of her.

"Don't be like that, big man," said Carmine, leaning his head around her skirts. He filched the crystal glass from Fancy's tray as he did so. "Drink some tea. You'll feel much better."

"I'd rather you didn't hurt him," Fancy remarked. "He complains such a lot when he's injured."

"How appallingly rude," said Carmine, sitting back with his champagne glass. "Fancy, you don't appreciate me. I appreciate you. You should learn to be more reciprocative."

Barric's shoulders relaxed a little. He could even have been smiling a little—it was hard to tell, with the scar that ran across his face—as he accepted the cup that Fancy proffered once again.

"Would you excuse us, lady?"

"Will you hurt him?"

"I think not."

As Carmine sipped from his glass, Fancy looked at Barric in silence. "Very well," she said, and swept out of the room again.

As the door closed behind her, Carmine said, in tones of outrage, "This isn't champagne! Fancy, where is my champagne? Fancy–!"

"Carmine," said Barric. "Out of respect for a lady, I will not pummel you until you tell me what I want to know. Instead, I will ask once again: Where is the shard?"

"How appallingly rude!" Carmine said again. "She waited until I was fearful of my life, and escaped before I knew what she'd done. Don't put the tea down, Big Man! I told you– I don't know *exactly* where it is. It could be in Avernse, or it could be in Montalier."

"Carmine–"

"I sent it off with someone," he added blithely. He took another sip of the liquid in his champagne glass, winced, and put it down again. "It was safer with her. As to what she's done with it, well, who knows? She's the sort to know what it is she's looking at– and if she doesn't, she tends to find out. Not like Fancy. Fancy is very restful that way: She does what you tell her to do—well, most of the time—and she doesn't ask uncomfortable questions."

Barric was silent for quite some time. When he spoke again, it was to say, more mildly: "Very well. There's nothing to be done about that. We'll have to begin with the others and go on from there. We could use you in the fight, Carmine."

"No, you couldn't," said Carmine frankly. "I'd get in the way and then be slaughtered messily. No, thank you."

"You used to be a lot more useful."

"That was before the Unseelie put spies in my canton," Carmine said, with a glittering, humourless smile. "It may surprise you to know, Big Man, that I'm now a marked Fae. If I go anywhere but my own Canton, I'll be fair game to any Fae with a sword or a spell quick enough."

"I see," said Barric. "In that case, we'll do what we can without you. I'll be off to the human world in two days: I'll come back before that, if I can."

"I'd rather you didn't, Big Man," said Carmine lazily. "I've done my part in this little game, and I'd rather live a peacefully cowardly life from now on."

"That's a shame," Barric said. If Carmine had been looking at Barric's face instead of at the glass in his own hand, he would have seen the grim sort of amusement there. "It would have been useful–"

"I don't like to be useful," Carmine warned. "I like to be comfortable."

"I wasn't talking about you," said Barric, and the amusement in his face had grown. "I was talking about Fancy. I'd take her with me if I thought she'd leave you."

Carmine sat bolt upright. "No! I won't have you trying to turn Fancy's head. She's mine, and she's not allowed to help anyone but me."

"Yes, she told me something similar," Barric nodded. "If you change your mind about helping–"

"I won't."

"–if you change your mind about helping, I'll be outside Harlech with the Llassarian princesses in two days' time. We've still several shards to find, and you've got a stake in this fight."

"No, I don't," said Carmine firmly. "I refuse to have a stake in it. I'm quite happy keeping my head down and pretending that those obvious little spies aren't really that obvious."

"Very well," Barric said. "Then I'll not see you again."

Carmine sipped at his drink again by accident, and grimaced. "I certainly hope not." He didn't rise when Barric nodded his farewell and ducked through the door: in fact, he didn't move for a good fifteen minutes, until an unwelcome thought seemed to occur to him. He bolted to his feet and strode from the room, hauling off his shirt as he went. "Fancy! Fancy!"

There was a distinct quietness to the marble hall, suggesting that any staff within earshot didn't dare to answer a summons that was not for them. Nor did Fancy appear in her usual prompt manner. Carmine, his eyes dangerously narrow, shouted again: "Fancy! If I have to come and find you–!"

"What will you do?" asked Fancy from behind him, in some interest.

Carmine spun. "Fancy! There you are!"

Fancy looked at him in a pained sort of way. "You couldn't keep your shirt on for longer than half an hour?"

"A physique as thoroughly gorgeous as mine shouldn't be hidden for longer than a moment," Carmine pronounced. "You're just lucky I choose to wear breeches, Fancy. I could walk around in my small-clothes and be considered a work of art. A work of art, Fancy!"

"I suppose I should be thankful for small mercies," muttered Fancy. "My lord, is Barric gone?"

"Yes, thank goodness!" He looked at her suspiciously and said: "He didn't try to take you with him?"

"He did, but I declined. I'm under oath to you."

"Is that why you didn't answer me when I called? You were rubbing shoulders with Barric?"

"I didn't answer when you called because I was attending to something else," said Fancy. "My lord, why would I ask if Barric had gone if he was talking to me? I would have known he was gone."

"What were you attending to?"

"I was changing," Fancy said.

Carmine's eyes flicked up and down her length. "So you were," he said, more mildly. "When did he try to convince you to accompany him, then, Fancy?"

"Earlier," said Fancy. "My lord, would you like me to assist you on with your shirt?"

"No, I wouldn't, Fancy! I won't be mothered! If I wish to stride about my domain naked, I have every right to do so!"

"Oh, good grief," muttered Fancy.

"And I won't have you *tut-tutting* at me under your breath, either."

"There's no reason to be cross with me because you're out of sorts with yourself, my lord," Fancy said. "Earlier, Barric mentioned that you might be leaving with him."

"Oh, he did, did he?"

"If you wanted to go with him, there's still time."

"I don't want to go with Barric."

"And there's no need to feel bad because you've refused to help your friend."

"He's not my friend. Barric is the *opposite* of friendly."

"And of course–"

"Fancy!"

"My lord?" Fancy's brows were raised, her expression just slightly enquiring.

Carmine stared at her in brooding silence for a few moments. He said: "I'm going back to bed."

FROM HIGH IN THE SKY, the Glasslight Canton is a thing of glittering beauty. There are the Wandering Hollies, for once meandering quite close to the castle, moonlight reflecting off their smooth leaves, and there is the Glass Mountain, a diamond-bright patch of reflected starlight and moonlight. There are the woodlands, which would be a vast sprawl of velvet darkness if it weren't for the network of pinpoint lights dancing in the dark, and all around that is the sudden and complete darkness of the next canton. There is the castle, right in the centre, with a single point of light gleaming bright into the sky—the crystal roof of the lord's bedroom suite—and there, all around the castle, that shifting mass of alternating silver and gold that is as large as a sea– *that* is the combined might of Seelie and Unseelie, brought to bear against the Glasslight Castle and Carmine, Lord of Glasslight Canto and Duke of the Wandering Hollies.

Within the castle, things are inclined to be darker. Carmine's bedroom, for instance, was deep in darkness, pierced only by the soft Faelight that was currently dangling from Fancy's fingers.

"I think you should get up, my lord."

A muffled voice said: "Don't be ridiculous, it's still dark."

"It generally is, in the Unseelie Cantons," said Fancy.

A groan. "Rub my temples for me, Fancy."

"I think not, my lord. You're not wearing a shirt, and you're inclined to be dangerous when you're not wearing a shirt."

Carmine opened one eye. "I'm usually without a shirt, I think you'll find, Fancy."

"Exactly, my lord," said Fancy. "You should perhaps take a moment to look out the window."

"Fancy," Carmine said silkily. Both eyes were open now, but they were distinctly narrow. "You made a certain oath to me when I brought you to–"

"Kidnapped," corrected Fancy.

"When I br– *kidnapped*? You wanted to come!"

"You didn't know that then. My lord, I really think you should look out the window."

"Regardless," said Carmine, with great coldness, "you made me an oath. You promised to be mine and obey me all your mortal life. I mention it because I think you've forgotten it."

"Oh no!" Fancy said, smiling faintly in the glow of Faelight. "I remember it very clearly. I was very careful how I worded it, so I'm quite sure. I made an oath in three parts: That I would serve you until death, that I would be only yours, and that I would always do what was best for you. Champagne for breakfast is *not* what is best for you, nor is encouraging you to lie abed or massaging your temples."

"Who is teaching all these humans how to make oaths?" demanded Carmine pettishly. He sat up. "Fancy, my head hurts!"

"I'm certain that the Fae don't get drunk," said Fancy. "That being the case, I can only imagine that your head hurts from pure contrariness. I will also add that there seems to be a rather large army gathered around the castle, and ask you yet again to come and see for yourself."

Carmine tumbled from the bed and to his feet in one effortless roll, his eyes bright and clear, and strode across to the window. That made Fancy smile again as she drew the curtains aside for him. "I see that you're awake, my lord."

Carmine's eyes flicked to hers for a silent moment, and then back to the seething silver and gold army below. "So it's begun," he said, beneath his breath.

"Some time ago, actually," said Fancy. "You've slept through most of it. I thought they could occupy themselves quietly outside without bothering us, but now they've started making a noise."

A deep, echoing crash from below bore out her words.

"Is that my front gate?"

"I imagine so," Fancy said. "I don't think they'll be able to break through it, though. You *did* reinforce it last cycle, didn't you?"

"Of course I did," said Carmine, though he looked slightly uneasy. He looked Fancy up and down, taking in her unchanged clothes, and added: "Haven't you been to bed?"

"No," said Fancy, edging aside the drapes with one finger to look at the mass below. "I've been rather busy."

"Fancy," said Carmine. "I'd like to know exactly how much you k–"

There was another crash from somewhere below stairs; heavy, bone-shaking, and certain. Fancy let the drapes drop. "You *didn't* reinforce the gate! My lord!"

Carmine cleared his throat. "It was an even chance either way. I *could* have done it, but then again, I *could* have decided that it was a lovely day and too nice to be spent in archaic and almost entirely useless magic."

"It doesn't seem so useless to me, my lord."

"Well, neither does it to me, now!" protested Carmine. "That's the benefit of hindsight, Fancy!"

Only by the smallest wince did Fancy betray her unease. "We should be going now, I think."

"A sensible idea," agreed Carmine. "We'd best take the secret passage: Follow me closely, or you'll get lost."

"Yes, my lord," said Fancy, and followed him from the room.

In the corridor, Carmine said frowningly: "It's too quiet. Where are the other staff?"

"I sent them away," Fancy said. "I didn't think you'd like for them to be killed."

"No," said Carmine, "but I'd really rather not be killed myself, Fancy! I can't help feeling that you might have thought of that before you sent away my guards as well. A dashing scar or two in the line of duty is all very well, but I have my face to think of, and I don't think the mass out there is interested in taking prisoners."

"Then you should have reinforced the gate when you said you were going to," said Fancy pointedly, throwing a swift glance over her shoulder. She added: "Besides, you don't need your guards: You've got me."

"That," said Carmine, with great coldness, "would be very useful if I were thinking of serving them tea or scolding them into submission. I'd rather have them dead enough not to hurt me, thank you. *This* way, Fancy."

They were scarcely three steps around the corner when two well-armed Fae turned into the same corridor and saw them. Carmine whitened, his fingers dripping with scarlet magic, and said: "Don't worry, Fancy. I'm sure my magic will get through their magic-resistant armour before they slaughter us."

"Carmine," said Fancy, with another of those momentary winces. "Please get out of my way."

It was perhaps her business-like voice that made the lord turn around. She had already unbuttoned the three buttons that lined her skirt at the left thigh, and was securing the material somewhere at the back. Carmine's dazed eyes took in, at one glance, the light boots, the breeches, and—most importantly—the twin knives that were sheathed to either leg.

"Fancy," he said. "This makes things very difficult for me."

"We'll talk about it later," Fancy said. "Behind me, please."

"With pleasure," said Carmine, and ducked behind her.

Fancy threw him a brief look over her shoulder. "Further away. These knives are longer than they look, and my reach is certainly longer than it looks."

The Fae weren't in a hurry. They waited, with faintly mocking smiles, while Carmine hastily stepped back a few paces further, and they even waited while Fancy drew her long knives.

"Give up pleasantly," said one of them. "You're good and hearty, and you've got a good set to you. You'll train well. We only want the traitor."

Fancy said over her shoulder: "I've never been particularly pleasant, have I, my lord?"

"Not particularly," agreed Carmine.

"There you go." Fancy smiled insincerely at both Fae. "And if it comes to that, the only way you're going to lay a finger on my lord is by going through me."

"Ah," sighed the Fae who had spoken earlier. "It's like slaughtering a good dog. Is the traitor worth your life?"

Carmine peered around Fancy's skirts. "I object to the term *traitor*!"

"Of course," said Fancy. "Isn't it the part of a good dog to die by its master's side? Will you begin, or must I?"

As leisurely as they had been before, were the Fae lightning fast when they had decided upon action. The first lunged forward, light and deadly, his blade darting for her heart, and Fancy spun in a scraping of blades. The Fae saw his blade slicked up and away just far enough to slice past Fancy's neck by a hair's-breadth, his eyes following as she curled in close with him, shoulder to shoulder, but he never saw the second blade that sliced off his head as Fancy completed her spin and embraced his shoulders from behind. The Fae's body stood still for a moment, held fast about the shoulders in the grim parody of a friendly embrace, before Fancy let it drop. The Fae's head bounced across the carpet, spurting blood, and came to rest at Carmine's feet.

"*Fancy!*" howled Carmine. "There is *blood* on my *breeches!*"

"I apologise, my lord," said Fancy, her knives moving very slightly in the air. She turned back to face the other Fae fully, her eyes locking with his, and he smiled.

"Come to me, sister," he said, and there was a surprised sort of respect to his voice.

This time, Fancy made the first move, a swift feint to the right that didn't shift the Fae. Instead, he caught her back-slashing left knife, disengaged, and shoved her backward. Fancy moved with the shove and landed lightly, her blades dancing at her sides and her knees just a little bent. Carmine, who had been caught in horrified fascination by the head at his feet, now forgot about it entirely and sat down with his mouth open to watch Fancy.

There wasn't a great deal left to watch: The second Fae followed his shove with a brief, slashing sally that bloomed red as Fancy cut through it with one knife and slid her second up and between his ribs at the side where his chest-piece ended. The Fae vomited blood and fell forward as Fancy stepped swiftly back, disengaging her blades. She nudged him with the toe of her boot, but he was already dead, so she wiped the blood away on his short cloak and resheathed her knives.

She looked expectantly at Carmine, but he was still gazing up at her, his face entirely fascinated. She prompted: "We should go, my lord."

"I think I'm in love," Carmine murmured.

"You can't be," Fancy said. "Remember that you don't fall in love with women who aren't beautiful. I could never match your plumage."

"That's true," agreed Carmine, "but isn't it the female who has the brown plumage, after all? You–"

"My lord," said Fancy. "There are at least three other windows along this hall. If there are going to be two Fae climbing through each of them, we'll shortly be outnumbered."

Carmine stood swiftly. "A very good point, Fancy. How many windows are there before we get to the stairs?"

"Too many," said Fancy, and led the way.

Still, there were no more Fae between them and the stairs, and by the time the crystal landing was in sight, Carmine let out a breath of relief. "The stairs," he said. "Nearly there, Fancy!"

"I think not," said Fancy, coming to a stop at the upper landing. Carmine, catching up with her, saw what she had seen: the hall below was already crowded with Fae. There were at least fifteen Fae there, mixed Seelie and Unseelie, and a good half of them were wearing the same magic-resistant armour that the other Fae had been wearing.

Fancy hissed regretfully. "Oh, that's unfortunate. Do stay behind me, my lord, and if it looks like they're about to surround me–"

"I'll jump into the hall and run for the passage alone, leaving you to die?" suggested Carmine pleasantly. "Thank you so much. Just what I was thinking." He leaned over the edge of the landing, and before Fancy could stop him, called out affably: "Isn't this a charming sight? Seelie and Unseelie working together for the good of Faery! So unlike the Seelie Fae earlier: They tried to steal a march on everyone by sneaking through a window. Tsk tsk. Shocking."

The two lead Fae looked at each other, silver glowering and gold suspicious, and then up at Carmine.

"You're lying, traitor," said the Unseelie Fae.

"We can throw you their heads, if you like," Carmine said. "Well, Fancy can. I don't like to touch them: they're a bit messy."

The Seelie Fae said, with the slightest glance at his Unseelie counterpart: "Seelie and Unseelie are working together."

"You should tell that to your men," Carmine pointed out. "They look very uncomfortable to me. Oh, look! That one seems to be drawing his sword."

It was the Seelie Fae furthest toward the back who moved first. His sword was already half-drawn, and as his hand wavered, the slightest sound of sword against scabbard rasped through the silent room. Swords were drawn in an instant, and the floor below became an instant *melee*, silver clashing with gold, and scarlet staining the whole.

"You're *welcome*, Fancy," said Carmine, and bowed. Fancy grabbed him by the wrist mid-bow and dragged him down the stairs, much to his protestation. "Fancy! Fancy, we're supposed to go *away* from the Fae with swords!"

"We need the passage," Fancy said tersely, slapping away a blade that came too close, and shoving Carmine behind her again. "This is the best chance we'll get. Quick!"

"Why do you know where the passage is?" groaned Carmine, tugged into a run again. "Am I master of this castle, or am I not?"

Fancy said soothingly: "Of course you are, my lord. Duck, please. Oh, sorry."

"Blood again! If this doesn't come out of my hair, Fancy–!"

"I'll wash it for you later," said Fancy, with a commendable lack of exasperation.

Carmine, brightening, said: "All right, then," and allowed himself to be pushed through the closest door without objecting.

"Quickly," Fancy said, dragging him across the room. "Whatever Fae are left of that lot will be after us as soon as they pick themselves up."

"It's all very well to say that when you've shut us into a room with only one exit," remarked Carmine. "But since you're suddenly a terrifying beauty with blades and know about my own personal secret escape passage, I suppose you have some way of getting us out of here."

"*Everyone* knows about your personal secret passage," muttered Fancy.

"Good heavens, not that one." Carmine looked at her more closely. "You don't know about the real one, then? What a relief! I was beginning to think I'd welcomed a spy to my bosom."

"You've always welcomed spies to your bosom," said Fancy. "You say it's the best place to keep them. And I do know about the other passage, but we haven't got time to get there."

"Then how will we escape?"

Fancy, who was busy pushing at spots on the wallpaper, said: "We won't. We're going to hide for a while, *then* we'll escape. There's another passageway closer by. Oh, here we go!"

Carmine stared blankly at the hole that had so suddenly appeared in the wall. "This isn't a passage. Not even for a brownie."

"That's what I just said," nodded Fancy. "We're going to hide. In you get, my lord. Squash up, please; we both have to fit."

"If we must, we must," said Carmine, wriggling his brows.

SILENCE. Silence and darkness. Outside the hidey-hole, Fae searched Glasslight Castle, magic seeking and searching through nooks and crannies, passing from room to room.

Inside the hidey-hole, the darkness remained, but the silence was broken.

"How long have you been serving me now, Fancy?"

A sigh. "Is it important, my lord?"

"I suppose not," said Carmine. "But I thought we might as well have some conversation if we're just waiting around to die."

"I've been serving you for five years now," Fancy said. "And we're not going to die. We're going to escape through to the human world and keep out of sight for a little while. I know that will be very difficult for you, but–"

"There's no need to make such a small space stuffy with that amount of sarcasm," Carmine protested. "I'm not sure I approve of your carrying knives, Fancy. It makes you too sharp."

"I was always sharp," Fancy said. "You only notice it more now because you thought my tongue was the only sharp thing about me."

"Patently false," declared Carmine. "I've always had an immense amount of respect for the sharpness of your elbows as well. Do you think they've gone? Shall I fetch us a little bit of light?"

"You might as well," said Fancy. "They won't be able to sense it with all the other magic that's going off in the castle at the moment. Goodness, they're being a bit loud, aren't they?"

"Other ma– *what* other magic?"

"All those little things I've been asking you to enchant for the past cycle," said Fancy. "It's like little firecrackers going off all over the castle. They've already stopped looking at the minor ones, I'll wager."

She leaned forward to press her ear against the wall opposite the hidden entrance, just barely avoiding Carmine's bare chest, and he said: "Not that I'm complaining, Fancy, but isn't the entrance on your side? If you wanted to get closer to me, you only had to ask. On a side-note, have you always smelled of cardamom, or is this a special occasion?"

"That's probably because of the knives, too," said Fancy callously. "I've heard it said that the senses become especially sensitive in the face of mortal danger. I'm wearing the same perfume I've worn since I was a little girl. And I'm listening to *this* side because *this* is the side we'll need to leave by."

Their eyes met for a moment, and Fancy looked away almost immediately, shifting position so that she was gazing at the darkness behind Carmine instead. By contrast, Carmine continued to gaze at Fancy, his eyes thoughtful and slightly speculative, and Fancy's shoulders grew tense.

At last, his fingers leaving little dots of red magic where they tapped against the floor of the hole, Carmine said idly: "On another side-note, why are so many Fae and so much magic passing this convenient little hole entirely by?"

Fancy gave the smallest snort, and relaxed infinitesimally. "Fae. Always thinking they're so clever. They're passing it by because they're looking for magic: Concealing magic, transport magic, tunnelling magic. They're not looking for mechanical entrances and exits because it never occurs to their brilliant and highly intelligent minds that anything unmagical can possibly be as good as something magical."

"I'd object, but it's true," remarked Carmine, and a small ribbon of ruby magic flared up between them. "Fancy, am I sitting on a pack?"

"Probably," said Fancy, without looking. She was still listening intently at the wall. "I pushed it in from this side, and you were first in."

"You had a pack in here, ready for us?"

"Ready for you. Do you mind not putting that flicker right in my face, my lord?"

"Yes, I do mind. You've been a very deceitful serf, and I want to see if you're hiding any more secrets."

Fancy continued to gaze at the space over his shoulder, ostensibly listening carefully. "I'm not hiding any more secrets. Check your pack to make sure it has everything you need."

"Unless it has champagne in it, I'm quite certain it doesn't," remarked Carmine, but he opened the pack with fingers that ran ruby with magic. "Where's your pack, Fancy?"

"I have everything I need with me," said Fancy, shifting slightly. "It's getting quieter out there, my lord. We'll be able to move soon."

Carmine, who was investigating the contents of the pack,

complained: "Why is there a shirt in this pack? You could have fit at least one bottle of champagne in here!"

"Because I was quite certain that you wouldn't have one on when it came time to run."

"When it came time to– and that reminds me! How long have you been colluding with Barric?"

"That?" Fancy took her ear away from the wall at last. "A few years now, I should think. He was worried that something like this would happen, and took me into his confidence. We've had reason to fight together once, so he knows what I'm capable of."

Carmine, indignantly, said: "You belong to me, Fancy, and I won't have you flirting with other Fae!"

"It was fighting, not flirting," Fancy said dryly.

"With Barric, that is flirting. You're not to fight with him any more."

"You're the one who told me to keep him from the door if he came again."

"Then I take it back," muttered Carmine. "Anyway, if the Seelie keep that lot up out there, it's not very likely I'll have a door to my name after today, so there's no reason for you to be keeping my door." An especially loud crash from somewhere in the extremities of the castle lent credence to his fears, and Carmine winced. By way of keeping his mind off the destruction outside, he said: "You've never told me why you decided to come with me that day, Fancy."

"You kidnapped me, my lord."

"Yes, I know *that*. But with the kind of irritating little charms you had sewn about your skirts and those knives—which I *assume*, Fancy, were hidden all the time in your petticoats!—you could have put up quite the struggle. You could have killed me without losing too many of those silver charms."

"No," said Fancy slowly. "I'm quite certain I couldn't have killed you. If it comes to that, my lord, why did you choose to take me? There were others in that room who were trying to break Parrin's curse– prettier by far than me, too. I was surprised that you chose me."

"Obviously I chose you because I'm a masochist," muttered Carmine. "I knew you wouldn't let me get away with things I shouldn't get away with, and you were so straight and tall that I wasn't afraid of falling in love with you. I was quite sure you weren't beautiful enough to tempt me."

Fancy gave a soft, unexpected snort of laughter. "I've always been useful that way. It was one of the considerations I had when I came with you. We can go now, my lord."

"Yes, but now things are more difficult," complained Carmine. "I was quite sure that you weren't beautiful, so I was quite sure I couldn't possibly be in love with you, but now I've seen you dance with the Fae. It's no use pretending you're not beautiful, now."

"We can go now, my lord," repeated Fancy.

"Yes, but now I don't *want* to go," said Carmine, a sparkling red trail of his magic slipping silkily around Fancy's wrist. "I want to stay and discuss–"

"*Carmine!*"

If there had been any remaining Fae in the next room, they would have seen a section of the wall mysteriously cave in on itself, and a shirtless Fae tumbling from the hole. They would have seen, moreover, a tall, flushed human woman climbing out behind him and unbuckling her sheathed knives from her legs as if absorbed by the task.

"What are you doing, Fancy?" demanded Carmine. "There's no reason to go drawing knives because I tried to kiss you. Let's not be over-dramatic."

"The irony of you referring to anyone else as over-dramatic–"

"I know," agreed Carmine. "Astounding, isn't it? *Darling* Fancy. Please don't kill me."

Fancy threw him an exasperated look. "The knives aren't meant to be sheathed at my legs," she said. "That's just where I've been keeping them so that no one could see them. I prefer a cross-draw from the back."

Carmine, not quite beneath his breath, said: "I liked them where they were." Louder, he added: "Where to from here, Fancy? I only ask since you seem to know the secrets of my castle better than I do."

"It's just down the hall, in the silver morning room," said Fancy, fastening the last buckle of her sheaths. She shrugged her shoulders to test the fit and nodded decisively. "That should do it, I think. My lord! Wait! I have to check the hall first!"

She was speaking to an open, empty door. Carmine, leaving his pack behind, had already wandered into the hall. Fancy muttered beneath her breath and scooped the pack up as she passed, stuffing Carmine's shirt back in. She followed swiftly, but not so swiftly that she didn't check the length of the hall, both ways, before entering the hall. The left was clear. To the right, a smiling Fae was softly stepping to move within throwing range of the oblivious Carmine, a knife already raised.

"Carmine!" shrieked Fancy.

Carmine, ducking instinctively, barely avoided the first knife. Fancy leapt for her lord, long and low, and tackled him to the ground with a solid thump, colliding with the wall. Carmine groaned, but Fancy gave him no time to bewail his wounds. Before either he or the Seelie Fae knew what was happening, she had Carmine up and through the doorway, panting.

"Bother!" she said, slamming the door. She looked left and right, and seized on a rather hefty easy-chair that was within reach, dragging it against the door. Outside, someone beat against the wood, shouting. "Now they know where we are. Quick, move as much furniture against the door as you can manage!"

"Fancy," said Carmine, his eyes very narrow, "you called me *Carmine*."

Fancy froze for the slightest moment, but made herself busy

the next by tugging a display cabinet against the door. "Are you sure, my lord? I don't think so. Do you think you could reinforce this with a little magic?"

"I'm very certain," Carmine said, his eyes glinting. "And you've done it three times, now. Fancy! Well, I never! That's tantamount to a declaration of love, from your dour little lips."

"We'll leave my lips out of this, thank you very much," Fancy said, with a very slight pinkness to her cheeks again. "My lord, a little magic, if you please!"

"All right," said Carmine, helping her to move another display cabinet as his magic made bloody veins over the door. "But I want to discuss this further, Fancy! Where's this passageway of yours?"

"Here," said Fancy, dragging another chair by its scrollwork top. Instead of taking it to the door, she kicked it into position against the left-hand wall. That done, she looked up and down the narrow room, measuring distance and looking with approval at the arrow-slits that were opposite the door, the only other opening in the room.

"That won't do much good," opined Carmine. "It's too spindly. What are you trying to reinforce over here, anyway?"

"It's not for reinforcing," Fancy told him, and rammed her right knife through the wallpaper. Ignoring Carmine's protests, she turned her wrist sharply, and a vast ticking of clockwork began behind the paper. A small hole began to form above the top of the chair, spiralling as it grew, and before long, it was an opening big enough for a reasonably big Fae to duck through. The tunnel beyond it was comfortably high, though the edges were rimmed with what looked suspiciously like iron.

Carmine watched with a grim kind of helplessness. "I would like to know how you got this in here without me knowing about it, Fancy."

"That was the easy part," said Fancy, glancing back worriedly at the door. The thumping and shouting had grown as more Fae beat at it, and there was already a distinct sense of magic working against Carmine's spell. "You'd best get in, my lord. The door won't hold for very long, and the passageway will close up again in a few minutes. Once it's closed, we won't be able to use it again."

"I have to say, Fancy, that it doesn't seem like a very useful passageway."

"It is if you're trying to escape from someone who can't get in," said Fancy. "It goes directly to the human world, by the way, so once you're out, you should be able to meet with Barric."

"Leaving aside for a moment my complete disinterested in meeting with Barric," began Carmine, "I would like to know why you keep saying 'you' and not 'we'."

"You'll have to mind the edges of the passageway, too," said Fancy. There was a very large *thump!* At the door, and the whole was edged with golden Seelie magic. "Just at the beginning here; they're iron. You'll need the chair to climb in."

"I saw that, thank you very much," Carmine said. "What I want to know is–"

"Climb in now, my lord," Fancy said, drawing her knives. "I can't keep you covered if you're running around the room like a cricket. I'd rather have you out of the way."

Carmine, muttering, did as he was told. He could see the spell that was working away at the door, and he knew better than Fancy how potent it was. Crouching at the entrance of the passage, just out of reach of the iron edges, he peered back into the room and said: "Why did you come with me that day, Fancy? You still haven't answered me. I know there was the whole *brouhaha* with your brother trying to marry you off, but I'm sure you could have stood up to him. You were already making plans to save that princeling from his fate."

"I could have," said Fancy, reinforcing the stacked furniture with one boot. "I was going to, actually. That day– that day when you arrived– it's what I was going to do. Are you sure you want to hear this, my lord? You won't like it."

"*Fancy.*"

"All right," Fancy said. Her shoulder was to him, her eyes on the door to their left, and her blades had already begun to move a little in the air. "I came with you because the first moment I saw you, I fell in love with you."

"Wait," said Carmine. "This isn't what I was expecting. Fancy, do you mean that you've been living with me for five years– that I've been so *careful* not to– and that– *Fancy!*"

"I'd never fallen in love before," said Fancy reflectively, her right foot edging forward in response to a particularly loud *crack!* "I was quite old, even then: Thirty years old and never married, or in love. It took me by surprise."

"Stop," said Carmine, his voice uncertain. "Stop it, Fancy."

"All right," Fancy said, smiling a little. "But you did ask, my lord. I warned you that you wouldn't like it."

"That's not what I meant. I meant– you're telling me this because you think you're not coming with me, aren't you?"

Fancy was silent for a moment. Then she said: "Perhaps the door will come down after the passage closes. Perhaps it will come down before. If it comes down before, I'll be here to guard the entrance until it closes safely."

Carmine, in exasperation, said: "I should have known! Of all the times to choose to tell me that you love– I won't be sacrificed to, Fancy!"

"If you try to come out, I'll only hit you on the head and put you back in," said Fancy, without looking around. "There's no sacrifice: There's no future for Fae and human couples, after all."

"Not a particularly long one," agreed Carmine. "But I've heard it's a sweet one."

"And when I'm white-haired and people think I'm your grandmother?"

"I'll be just as frightened of your sharp knives and sharper tongue," said Carmine promptly. "How will we know the passage is about to close?"

"It'll start ticking," Fancy told him. There was another crack, and this time, they could see the glimmer of Seelie and Unseelie through the door. "That will be the clockwork starting up again."

"I'll call out to you when it starts," Carmine said. He was breathing too quickly, the breaths ragged and short. "Make sure you're close, Fancy. If you're not close enough, I'll jump out again and give the Fae a merry little chase around the room before I die."

That did make Fancy look around. "Don't make me hit you on the head, Carmine."

"Try it," invited Carmine.

The door cracked one last time, a groaning creak that it was, and Fancy snuffled a small, exasperated laugh. She turned and darted for the passage too quickly for Carmine to do more than instinctively raise one hand in protection, and kissed him full on the mouth. Carmine overbalanced onto the seat of his breeches, and was too slow to snatch her back and reciprocate in full: Fancy was already back in position between the passage and the door, and meeting the first of the Fae as they came through the splintered door.

Carmine, his face white, watched every slash and pivot intently, counting with a concentration amounting almost to despair, the number of Fae struggling through the stricken door. He was so intent upon the fight and the count, in fact, that when the *tick-ticking* began, he heard it only as an answer to the counting in his head. It was when the amount of Fae in the room became constant, and yet the count in his head still continued, that he half-stood, convulsively.

"Fancy!"

Fancy, through her teeth, panted: "Just...a moment...my lord!"

"There are no more moments," said Carmine, and he seemed surprised by the sound of his own voice, so grey and dry. "Fancy,

I refuse to be shut in a draughty passage without you! If you don't come along at *once* I will never again wear a shirt. I'll flirt with every woman I meet! I'll– I'll– Fancy, I need you to wake me up in the mornings and refuse to massage my temples! I *order* you! *Fancy–!*"

Clockwork *tick-ticked* faster and faster, and began to whirr. Fancy, sweeping a circle around her with blood-stained knives, darted forward, driving back the assembled Fae with her indiscriminate slashes, then turned on her heel and ran for the narrowing passageway. It was too small, but she leapt for it anyway, long and lean, and something scarlet and warm wrapped around her, and pulled her through...

A CLEARING IN THE WOODS: quiet, cool, and peaceful. All is as it should be– except for the circling maw that is gradually opening wider somewhere toward the edge of the clearing.

"Light, glorious light!" carolled a voice.

"That's not a very Unseelie sentiment, my lord."

"I'm not a particularly Unseelie Unseelie, if it– are you quite well, Fancy? You shouldn't cough like that."

"I was surprised," said Fancy dryly. "There are the stairs, my lord. Take care not to let the sun glare too much in your eyes at first."

"Thank you, Fancy, I *have* visited the mortal realm before, after all," said Carmine, emerging from the earth with the air of an immortal gracing the world with his unworldly beauty. Around the clearing, branches squeaked together and leaves whispered against each other, drawing closer to the Fae presence that was Carmine.

"Good grief," said Fancy, staring around as she followed him. "Isn't it enough that nearly every woman you meet throws herself at your feet?"

Carmine said smugly: "Don't be jealous, Fancy: I like you best. This place, though. I quite like it. We'll come back here again."

Fancy, who had dropped to one knee to clean her knives, said into the knife-reflection of herself: "Will we?"

"Yes, we will!" Carmine said. "The trees *like* me. I like to be liked. I'll build a house here. Perhaps my hollies will wander through."

"*You'll* build a house?"

"Well, perhaps we can find a needy brownie or two, and convince it to help out. After all the death and war and destruction, of course. Speaking of death, war, and destruction, when are we supposed to meet up with this young princess and the Big Man?"

"Tomorrow," said Fancy. "Outside Harlech. If we want to meet with them, we should get started."

"I'd rather kiss you again," Carmine suggested.

Fancy's hand didn't cease its polishing. "And the princess and Barric?"

"We'll walk quickly."

"My lord, I–"

"Carmine," prompted Carmine.

"My lord–"

"Fancy, I insist upon being called *Carmine*. You promised–"

There was a sliver of silence where Fancy considered her oath, and sighed. "Carmine, I told you before: There's no future for us. There never has been. I've accepted it, and I'm quite happy with it."

Carmine gave her a disgruntled look. "Is that so? Well, I'm not particularly happy with it, and you made an oath–"

"To obey, to be yours, and to do the best for you," nodded Fancy. "If the first contravenes the third, I have every right to do as I think best. I was very–"

"Yes, yes, you were very careful about how you worded it," Carmine complained.

"I was," agreed Fancy. "I've seen the result of Fae and human coupling, and that was a coupling where they loved each other. I'll not do that to you."

"And your oath means doing everything that is good for me regardless of how I feel about it."

Fancy smiled a little. "That's right."

Carmine, his eyes very bright, said: "So what you're saying is that so long as *you're* human and *I'm* Fae, there's no hope for an *us*?"

"Exactly," said Fancy, sliding her long knives back into the sheathes that criss-crossed her back. Her face had closed once again.

"Well, then," said Carmine. "That's easy."

There was a distinctly worried line to Fancy's brow. "What does that mean? What are you planning, Carmine?"

"Never you mind," Carmine said, his eyes still alight with mischief. "You'd only try and stop me. You just mind your oath and let me worry about my own plans."

Fancy looked at him for some time, and there was a fond kind of amusement in her eyes. She said: "I don't think you have a plan."

"Then I'm happy to tell you that you're quite wrong, Fancy!" said Carmine, and kissed her. "Right now, I'm going to kiss you again. No, don't hit me, or I'll cry."

There was a brief scuffle, which ended with Carmine on his back in the grass, regarding the sky, and Fancy some distance away, looking conscious.

Being upended didn't seem to have impaired Carmine's good humour. He said to the sky: "Later on, I'll probably kiss you again."

"You won't," warned Fancy, looking even more conscious.

"I will," said Carmine dreamily. "I'll even let you hit me–"

"Let me– *let* me hit you?"

Magnanimously, Carmine said: "Let's not quibble, Fancy.

Couples in love shouldn't quibble. I'll let you hit me if it makes you feel better, but kisses there must be. And by the time we've finished finding the pieces of this atrociously outdated sword, you're going to agree to marry me."

THE END...
...REALLY